HER DEEPEST

Desire

SAKSHI KAPOOR

LAUNCHPAD

An imprint of
Srishti Publishers & Distributors

Srishti Publishers & Distributors

212A, Peacock Lane

Shahpur Jat, New Delhi – 110 049

editorial@srishtipublishers.com

First Published by Launchpad,
an imprint of Srishti Publishers & Distributors in 2024

First digitally published by
Srishti Publishers & Distributors in 2020

HER
DEEPEST
DESIRE

Shruti finished her cardio exercises and thought of heading home. Shruti was a twenty-six-year-old petite single woman living in Delhi. She was obsessive about her body, having battled extra pounds through her younger years. Her current slim body was due to all the time in the gym shaping herself.

Shruti's had a curvaceous and desirable body, with the right assets, especially her derriere, that got her many looks that her boyfriend, Raj, got very jealous about.

Shruti met Raj through a common friend and they have been dating for a year now. She had a routine life of a 9-5 corporate job, followed by intense workout. She was living alone in the big-city, with her parents settled comfortably in their hometown. She lived independently and while she had everything she wished for in material comforts; she was looking forward to taking the next big step in her love-life – that towards commitment to someone she wanted to spend the rest of her life with.

While her weekdays were hectic and work-oriented, she spent her weekends with Raj. Shruti had been happy with her life and relationship in the initial phase, but just a few months ago she had started feeling restless due to the monotony of their relationship. She thought it had got a bit stale and repetitive. The same old routine of weekdays and weekend was no longer exciting for her. Her heart desired for something new.

Shruti reached home when she got a call from Raj.

"My school buddy, Arjun, is coming to India tomorrow. He will be staying with me for this weekend," Raj announced over the call. "You know, Arjun and I were high school teammates in the football team and he was a star player of our school. He left for his graduation abroad after school and has been working there ever since. We barely got to catch up a couple of times since then," he added, remembering his old days.

Shruti had already heard this multiple times from Raj and also that Arjun is a lady's man. However, she was not thrilled about this, as she never really liked any of his friends that she had met.

The next day, when Shruti finished her crunches, she saw four missed calls from Raj. There was one message that read '*Sorry for disturbing you from your favourite cardio time. But had this emergency. I have an important meeting today till five in the evening. I had promised Arjun that I will be there to receive him at the airport. But I am stuck now. Sweetheart, please do me this favour and pick him up. I am sending you his flight details. You can drop him at my flat and hang around till I reach. Love you…*'

It was already 12:10 p.m. and Arjun was supposed to arrive at 1. It would take at least half an hour to reach the airport and she had no time to take a shower and change her clothes.

The flight landed at 1 p.m. Shruti pulled up looking for a man not knowing much more. She was in her gym clothes, having come directly from the gym. She decided to get out of the car to have a better look. She had on her tight workout pants showing off her ample ass and tight tank top that showed off her nice bouncy bosom.

Arjun approached Shruti, all suited and booted.

"Hi, if I am not wrong, you are Shruti, Raj's girlfriend." Shruti raised her one eyebrow, staring at him. "Oh sorry, forgot to introduce myself. I am Arjun." Arjun introduced himself and casually looked at her up and down.

"Hello! Welcome to India," Shruti said with a fake smile.

Arjun stepped forward and gave her a light hug. Shruti rolled her eyes at his unexpected behaviour. They got into her car and he just kept talking about himself. Of course, Shruti could feel his eyes looking down her tight tank top. He was totally checking her out. She was a little disgusted but a little pleased as well by the attention.

Shruti found Arjun different from Raj's other friends. Arjun was witty and loquacious, and she loved talking to him and getting all his attention. They finally got back to Raj's apartment. Shruti ordered lunch while waiting for Raj to come back from the meeting.

"Raj will come after five in the evening and we will go out for drinks and dinner. You must be tired, so you can rest meanwhile." Shruti tried to excuse herself.

However, Arjun said, "I don't need a nap per se. However, I think I will take a quick shower and freshen up. Can you show me the way to the bathroom?"

As Shruti walked towards the guest bathroom, Arjun was checking her out. She could feel his eyes on her and knew he was cooking something naughty in his mind. She decided to ignore the feeling, as she was enjoying the attention. Whilst Arjun went in for his shower, Shruti ruffled through the clothes she kept at Raj's place. Since she had spent quite a few nights over, she had an extensive wardrobe here.

Suddenly she heard a loud grunt of pain from the guest room and hurried towards the room. She saw Arjun holding a towel to his waist while massaging his ankles. He looked at her sheepishly and said, "Sorry, I bumped by ankle really hard on the bed. Did not mean to scare you."

Shruti was swept away by the physique on display in front of her. While Raj was a fit, good-looking man when they started dating, he had let go of his fitness a long time back. Here was a man who was all fit, hard and strong - right in front of her. She could feel something inside her wake up. She had not felt this feeling in a long time.

Her relationship with Raj had been monotonous for a long time now. They were barely talking and expressing their love to each other and mostly spent their time together at clubs or bars, which did not lead to them progressing further to a meaningful relationship. She wanted more and wondered if Arjun was the man for it. However, she shunned those naughty thoughts away and said, "The medical box is in the kitchen. Let me know if you need something?" Arjun waved her away, saying it was nothing.

Shruti wanted to get away from this situation, where she was feeling new emotions teeming inside her. She said, "I think I will catch a small nap. Maybe you can rest too?" She went back to Raj's bedroom and fell into a restless sleep. She woke up a few hours later to laughs and yelling from her boyfriend and Arjun. Shruti could hear Arjun say, "Lucky man! Your girl is so beautiful".

She freshened up before joining both the boys. She saw Raj and Arjun gulping beers and watching TV. She knew if they had to follow up with their plans, she needed these two guys to get moving.

"Raj, we need to get ready. It's almost 7 p.m." Raj had a standard weekend planned for his buddy - clubbing on Saturday and brunch on Sunday. The boys immediately followed her and they all started to get ready.

Shruti put on her newest teal dress that she bought a couple of weeks ago. She had kept it at Raj's for the weekend and was glad to try it out. After all, she was going to be showing off for not one but two studs this weekend. The neck plunged all the way down to her ample bosom, accentuating them. The dress was thigh high. Shruti loved to dress in the latest fashion for the club. It made her feel nice and sexy and it would be easy access for Raj when they got home drunk. She had her makeup all done and put on her heels. Her raven hair was open and dropping to the back of her waist.

When they got to the club, it was starting to warm up. They sat at a table in the club playing truth or dare.

"So first it's Shruti's turn. Truth or dare?" Arjun asked. "Dare!" She knew that he would want to know something naughty if she said the truth. While she was completely naughty in bed, she never liked people taking liberties with her.

"Are you sure?" Arjun asked.

"I am never unsure." She assured.

"So, let me start with an easy one. You have to go to that bartender and have to flirt with him to get a free drink. Can you do this?" Arjun dared her.

However, she had never done something like this before, but accepted this challenge. She pulled her dress down in the front a little. She went over to the bartender, who came right to her.

"What can I get for you?" He asked. Shruti twirled her hair and passed a naughty smile, looking into his hazel eyes.

"Three tequila please." Bartender was back to her with her drinks.

"How much?" She asked in a flirtatious voice.

"Just keep coming back to me, beautiful," he replied.

Shruti came back to applause from the table.

Now it was Arjun's turn.

"So, what would you choose, Mr Arjun, truth or dare?" Raj asked.

"I love to share my secrets." Arjun winked. "Truth!" he said.

"I want you to tell us the number of girls you have been with." Raj asked. They all laughed.

"I have dated eight girls, and hooked up with eleven girls who I didn't date," Arjun replied.

"Can't believe the numbers." Raj and Shruti denied to accept Arjun's answer.

Shruti knew he was supposed to be a big playboy,, but that had to be a lie. The game was still on till Raj was loaded and was being a mean drunk like he can be at times. However, Shruti was in the mood for a dance and insisted her boyfriend to dance with her. Raj, in his sloshed voice, asked Arjun to dance with her since he wasn't much of a dancer. Arjun agreed, as he was waiting for this proposal and soon, they were out dancing on the dance floor among everyone. Arjun was a great dancer, and they were dancing to club music.

Shruti loved it when men could dance and she was enjoying dancing with each other. Arjun put his hand on her waist and pulled her a little closer. They slowly started grinding on each other. While this was unexpected and Shruti was getting worked up, she didn't react much. She saw he was getting excited and being curious, she decided to rub up against his cock. Shruti wanted to give him a cheap thrill and also check out his package, to see where the myth ended and reality started. However, she was shocked at the size she felt. She wasn't , so she had to feel it again. She slid against him and grinded against him once again. Yup, he was more than the myth and it was all man down there.

The feeling of Arjun's hard body against hers was heavenly. Shruti lost herself to it. She looked around, but not seeing Raj held Arjun's hand and took it over to her waist. They were soon pressed close together. Her bossom pressed hard against his chest and his cock pressed firmly on Shruti's pussy. She felt a thrill shoot through her body, something she had never felt before. This was something she desperately wanted.

Shruti was sure that Raj could not see them. They came closer, and she rested her head on Arjun's shoulders while he leant forward to kiss her neck. His hands slowly went up and felt Shruti's tits from the side and she just held Arjun tighter, as they both moved in slow, romantic dance steps. She didn't encourage him, but she didn't want to stop him either. He lifted her face and looked into her eyes. Shruti could see the promise of pleasure in his eyes.

He whispered in her ears, "Shruti, I want to satisfy all your needs, all your desires. But tell me no and I will stop."

She said, "Don't stop honey."

Arjun kissed her passionately. They were tightly enmeshed in each other's embrace. Soon she was facing the wall as he turned her around and held her from behind, and his cock was deeply planted into her ass. He was massaging her buttocks from outside, and she was just loving it. In a short while, Arjun took her hand and had her put it behind her ass. She grabbed him from outside and pressed his cock into her hand.

Shruti slowly started touching his big cock and stroked it through his jeans while moving her ass in a dirty, naughty motion. They kept grinding on each other and he kept rubbing her ass on it. She could hear him breathe deep. He was so turned on, so was she. As the song ended, they went back to check on Raj. Raj was super drunk and creating a fuss. Security was kicking him out for being too drunk and creating a ruckus.

Arjun grabbed him and threw Raj over his shoulder. She was amazed at Arjun's casual show of core strength. He had the body of a Greek God. She was definitely more turned on than she had ever been.

Shruti was pissed at her boyfriend, so she told Arjun just to throw Raj in the back seat and she wasn't going to deal with him tonight. Arjun was able to drive, since he only had a few drinks. Raj passed out before they got home. While waiting at a traffic light, Arjun told her about how he had never danced with such a sexy woman.

Shruti told him that she had never danced with a man that could move like that. Arjun then reached over and touched her left nipple through her dress. Her pussy was dripping wet, and he then touched her other nipple. She glanced back to see Raj passed out. All she could think of was the size of his cock when they were dancing. She took his hand and sucked on his thumb.

She pushed his hand between her legs. He slipped in one of his fingers and then two. She then took his hand and sucked her juices off his fingers. She loved seeing his dark hands on her tanned white body. They hit a stretch of empty dark road and they started making out. He was such a great kisser. She reached for his pants. She undid his belt buckle and then his zipper, never breaking their kiss.

He looked up and guided the car into an empty side lane. She rubbed the enormous bulge in his boxers. He said, "I saw the disbelief on your face when you touched it in the bar. You are going to believe it now."

She unbuttoned the button on his boxers and out sprung his large organ. His manhood was really long and as thick as her wrist. He wasn't even fully hard. She let out a gasp in surprise.

He said, "Do you believe now?"

She nodded sheepishly. Then her sexual instincts took over. Shruti licked his shaft from top to bottom, then teased him with her hot and wet tongue on the head, rubbing his balls.

She then worked her way up and down with her tongue swirling around. She finally took him all the way in her mouth. He pulled back her hair and then moved his hand back to her head, pushing her down. Shruti was in ecstasy, bobbing her head up and down on this stud.

She then stroked the shaft up and down and opened her oesophagus and began deepthroating him, letting him in as far as she could go, while licking the base of his hard manhood with her tongue. Arjun felt waves in his whole body. He then grabbed her by her hair and led her up and down the length of his cock. Shruti loved that Arjun took control. She was turned on to the maximum and loved every moment of it.

She was even more turned on to know they were on a road and someone might catch them. She went twice as fast and sucked that dick like a real pro. She then felt his cock tense up. She never swallowed,, but that was all she wanted to do when it came to this stud. Suddenly, the largest load Shruti had ever felt filled her mouth, and it leaked out of her mouth while she swallowed as much as I could.

Arjun moaned as he said, "You liked sucking that big dick, didn't you?"

She replied with a nod while she cleaned the cum off her lips. Arjun told her, "I'm going to make love to you many times."

She wanted a real man like Arjun to be inside her pussy. Arjun continued to play with her pussy and nipples on the way back home.

They helped Raj back into bed and she went to settle him for the night. Raj was asleep and Arjun was sleeping in the guestroom. All Shruti could think about was getting that large cock in her pussy and mouth as she tucked Raj into bed. Raj was asleep and she couldn't stop thinking about the big cock in the guest room.

She slipped out of the room and walked into the guest bedroom. There was Arjun, lying on his back nude without any covers. Shruti was drawn to this man. She slipped into the bed and put her mouth around his cock and started working on his cock and balls. He woke up and said, "It's about time I've been wanting that tight pussy of yours."

Shruti slipped off her teal dress and showed off her pink nipple and her clean bud. She kept working on his rod, taking it in deep while he held her hair with one hand and massaged her boobs with the other. He then suddenly pulled her over his face and her flower to his mouth. She was on top of him, working on his hard manhood while he was sucking her core. They were orally pleasuring each other at the same time, and she loved the feeling. He had such a large tongue and active fingers. He found her g-spot soon and before she knew it, she was cumming.

Shruti left his monster cock and turned to face him. She was on top and straddled his monster cock that she craved. She lowered herself onto his dick slowly. She got about a few inches in and she could feel her pussy already being stretched.

The sharp pain was only superseded by the excitement and pure pleasure. He slowly worked in his cock inch by inch. All the time his hand playing with her nipples. When he got his entire cock in, she cried out with her hand over her mouth. He was touching places inside her pussy that Raj had never touched. Shruti went into a moaning frenzy.

He moved into her bud hard and urgent as she bobbed up and down on his shaft. She leaned forward so that he could kiss her soft boobs and play with her engorged nipples. She gave him a deep bite on his neck and then his chest. She could feel him tense up and cum inside her moist, stretched pussy.

She asked Arjun, "How does that pussy feel?" as she broke into her second orgasm. He came inside her at the same moment, but he was still hard.

He said, "It's the tightest pussy I have ever felt."

She fell to the bed and embraced him. She looked at him and said, "I have never cheated on Raj, but with you, I couldn't resist."

Arjun replied, "I am glad you did. You are the hottest girl I have ever been with."

She languidly put her left leg over his waist as she started stroking his chest and kissing the strong, well-built chest. He then grabbed her hips and continued to move her soft thigh back and forth on his cock. She could feel his cock getting harder again under her soft thighs. She moaned, thinking of that hard cock.

Arjun looked into her eyes and said, "Shruti, I know what moves are in Raj's repertoire and I am sure you are bored with them. He is very straight laced and does only a few traditional moves. While I am more adventurous. Would you like to try something different?" Arjun leaned forward and whispered something naughty in her ears.

She shivered in her soul, knowing that what he was asking was going to be sinfully pleasurable. This was definitely the best sex ever. She was out of her mind. She pulled herself off of him, sat up on the bed and leaned her ass towards him. He understood that she had agreed, and then he turned her around and massaged her ass slowly and softly. He suddenly slapped it lightly, making her cheeks go red and then massaged them again. She moaned his name and bit her lip. She knew she was up for a hell of a ride. He stretched her cheeks and slowly opened up her cave, feeling it up for the first time. She had never felt this way before. It was a unique experience for Shruti, as she had never done this and especially with someone so big.

Arjun said, "Shruti, I need you to unclench your butt if you want to enjoy this" and kept massaging her.

She responded to his calm voice and gentle massage and relaxed even more. Soon his hands had opened her up wider. As the rubbing and massaging continued, she could feel a separate sense of pleasure. Suddenly Arjun took his long rod and buried his member between her cheeks, entering where no one had ever gone before.

Shruti cried out as his huge member entered her tight butthole and moaned his name. She could feel every inch of his manhood dig into her soft rear. He was half way though, and she was already full and too tight. Arjun moaned her name and said, "Ohh, Shruttiii, don't tighten up now. I want you to feel the pleasure you have never felt before."

His hands were massaging her butt, and she loosened up again, giving him space to bury more of his member into her. She could hear and feel his balls slapping her ass as he plunged deeper into her. This was clearly the best sex she'd ever had.

The feeling of initial pain was replaced by pleasure she had only dreamt of in a long time. This was a feeling like never before. Arjun held her heart-shaped ass in one hand, massaging and slapping it alternately, while his other hand snaked up to her shoulder. He held her by her shoulder and pulled her closer, burying himself even deeper. She moaned in a frenzy, not caring to be quiet anymore. She then came again, once more for the night, in a shower of orgasm. Raj had never got her to cum more than twice in one night.

She now knew she had never been with a real man till now and she was feeling the difference. She moaned out, "I want your cum on my ass cheeks. I want to feel your seed all over my round bum."

He then picked up the pace, and they both moaned in ecstasy as he cummed all over her. She then rolled over, and they held each other. She told her lover that she didn't want him to leave on Sunday. He said that he wanted to make love to her everyday till he was here, but he had to leave soon.

They lay together in a tight embrace till the wee hours of the night. Shruti went back to her bedroom in the morning and slept next to her boyfriend, while her lover slept in the bedroom.

Next morning Raj woke up with a hangover. Raj had blacked out and was wondering what he missed. Shruti filled him in on everything — well almost everything. She told him that they came back home as a couple and did what they did every weekend, which seemed to satisfy Raj. They went out and fixed breakfast for them and their guest. Arjun joined in soon enough.

Shruti told Arjun that he would have to come back soon, as they all had the best time yesterday. Raj suddenly said, "We should all plan for a Goa trip. We will have all the booze, beach, and babe one can ask for."

Shruti replied with a naughty smile, "Looks like I will be enjoying more soon."

A NIGHT
OF
PLEASURE

It was the month of February. It was Friday night, and I had planned to spend it at the recently opened swanky club in Gurgaon. The club was packed to its capacity, and the DJ was belting out hits as the crowd went crazy on the dance floor. Warm, nubile, sweaty bodies were pulsating and singing and dancing to the tunes of the beats under the intoxication of liquor and maybe something a bit stronger. In a haze of smoke and crowd, I noticed a shining diamond – Rachna – standing out from the crowd around her.

I knew Rachna from a previous organization where we used to work in the same team. All our team members were good friends, and we used to hang out a lot together after office, usually club-hopping or just chilling.

However, after I left that company more than a year back, I lost touch with all of them. But it was a surprise to see her in the pub all alone, without her boyfriend Rahul, who was also a part of our group in the office. We had been a team of five people and had been great friends. While I was the senior-most in terms of experience, we had always hung out as equals, or so I felt. Rachna was of average height and had a taut body, with a heavy bosom and a thick derriere. I always found her very attractive, and we had a casual, cool, and friendly rapport. However, she and Rahul started dating around the time I left the company, hence closing any chance of a future relationship with her.

When I saw her in the pub sitting at the bar alone, I was quite surprised. Anyway, I went ahead and said, "Hi Rachna! How are you? Long time."

Rachna was amazed to see me there, and jumped up. "Hey hi…" she responded and hugged me.

"I am so glad to see you after so long," I said. I was really happy to see her there.

"Yes, it is such a surprise to see you here. It's been ages since we last met. I am sorry for not being in touch. However, considering how things were when you left the company…." Rachna trailed off, not able to finish the sentence.

"It's okay, Rachna. I understand," I said, as I put my hand gently on her left elbow. "I am just glad to see you after so long. Let's get a drink, if you don't mind?" I said as I guided her towards the bar.

"Yeah, sure, let's get a drink. I was waiting for a friend, but she has not shown up yet," Rachna said as we moved towards the bar.

I asked the bartender to pour us a couple of tequila shots. "Noo… Not tequila… You know it is my weakness," said Rachna.

"And that's why you are so much more fun after a couple of shots down your throat," I said, as I passed on the shot glass to her. We had two shots of tequila in quick succession, the burning sensation hitting our throat, and soon, our senses too. I asked the bartender for an LIIT for Rachna and got a whisky for myself as we moved back towards the dance floor.

"So, what's new with you guys? How is Rahul?" I asked, feigning interest in Rahul, while my real interest was Rachna.

"Oh, we are doing great. We got engaged about four months ago, after he got promoted to senior team lead. I have been going crazy since planning for the wedding in November. You have to come. You can't miss it," said Rachna.

"Sure, I will try to make it for sure. I can't imagine missing out on such a momentous occasion." I said, as I slipped my hand up her arms again, pulling her closer, so that we could hear each other properly over the din of the loud music.

Rachna asked me, "What are you up to these days? We never heard from you."

"Well, after last year, I was not really in the mood to work in the same industry. I branched out into the security and surveillance industry and it turned out they valued my years of experience. I am now a Vice President and effectively running the whole operations," I said.

"Oh wow! You are Mr Big Shot now!" said Rachna and I could visibly see a change in her interest in me.

"Yeah, business is good. In these times of rising crime rates and terrorism, we have both corporate and government contracts."

However, changing tracks, I asked her, "Have you come here with somebody? I am surprised to see you alone."

She said, "No yaar, I came alone. However, I was supposed to meet my friend Simar here but seems like she ditched me. I was about to leave when you walked up to me."

I asked, "But why did you come all alone? I am sure Rahul would not be happy to stay away from you."

She said, "I wanted some time off from the office crowd, from the same old bitching and politics. Also, Rahul has been working late these days as he has more responsibilities as the senior team leader. But it's great we met."

"I agree. This was a stroke of luck," I said.

Without wasting any time, I offered her to dance with me. Rachna hesitated a bit, and I prompted her, "For the sake of the good old days. Come on! We used to have so much fun dancing."

She looked a bit torn, but then agreed with a nod and a smile.

We went to the dance floor and started dancing. I always knew that she was an amazing dancer, and we always moved well on the dance floor. We started with a slow tempo, slowly matching up to the tempo of the foot-tapping music, which was playing out loud. Soon we were moving fast, our bodies at ease with each other, as we used to dance back then. I had my hands around her waist while her hands were on my shoulder and back. I twirled her with my arms and her back was towards me while she shook her body to the music. The tequila had hit the spot by then and the cocktail after had loosened up both her limbs and the inhibitions. We were moving sensuously and smoothly against each other on the floor. I pulled her closer to me, holding her by her waist as she got close to me while dancing. Our bodies were rubbing against each other, and I was rubbing my manhood against her ass. Rachna could feel it, but she said nothing and pressed against me. I took that as tacit approval and pulled her closer in my arms. Taking advantage of the situation, I also moved my hands freely all over her body, touching her bosom and caressing her round, soft rump.

I turned her around and looked into her eyes. Rachna was quite high, but I could see that she was aroused as well, naked lust sparking in her grey eyes. I pulled her to me and hugged her while her breast got crushed against my chest.

She asked me, "Can we go and sit on a couch?"

I said, "Sure, let's go and sit in that corner. We will be able to talk, away from the noise." The corner in question was on one side of the pub, quite dark and away from the eyes of the people on the main dance floor.

We went and sat on the couch and she sat next to me, her legs touching and almost over my legs. I was still holding her by her waist and one of her hands was around me as well. I pulled her into a hug and she hugged me back in a tight embrace. My hard chest pushed against her breasts. My right hand moved downwards and caressed her naked thighs while my left hand held her against my body. She kissed me on my neck and I knew we were moving towards a point of no return. I rubbed her thighs and slowly slid my hand upwards, inside the hem of the short dress that she was wearing.

She was a little high and was enjoying the moment, kissing my neck and lips while my hands inched upwards on her thigh. All of a sudden, she brought her face very near to mine, and we locked our lips. We were kissing each other, lips darting in and out, while enjoying the background music. My body ached with the need I felt for her. All this while I was fondling her body, with one hand on her bosom and the other on her thighs, all the way up till her panties. She moaned and leaned against me.

The moment we finished kissing, Rachna asked me a question which I was expecting. She asked, "Let's get out of here?"

I said, "Definitely, let's go on a drive and then have a nightcap at my place."

We cleared the bill and headed towards the car parking in the basement.

She asked me if anybody would be home. I told her, "I live alone Rachna. You remember that we did go to my place after a lot of after-parties, after all?"

We got into the car and I started driving. My house was about three miles from the pub and the road to my apartment was quite dark and lonely. Ours was probably the only car on that road that night. As soon as we got on the road leading to my house, she put her hand on my thighs and rubbed over the cloth. She then ran her hand over the crotch and unzipped my denims. I was surprised and excited to see how desperate she was. My shaft was ready and engorged like a monster.

While I was driving, Rachna took my manhood out of my jeans. My length sprang up. She looked at my monster and immediately grabbed it.

"This looks yumm," she said while swiping her thumb over the shaft and bowed down to lick the tip with her tongue. The touch of her swollen, wet lips sent a shiver across my body. She slowly licked it from the base to the shaft and then took the mushroomed tip in her mouth slowly, while her hands moved up and down. A moan escaped from my mouth.

With her hand on the base of my penis, she slowly worked her way back up. She was tracing her wet lips with my stiffness and then slowly took me into her mouth all the way in and then pulling away slowly, hollowing her cheeks and sucking harder. I was trying hard to concentrate on my driving, as she was already driving me crazy. I decided to park my car on the road side. She slowly started swallowing my member and soon it was completely in her mouth as she let go of her hand. She increased the speed of her hand, gliding up and down while sucking and swirling the tip with its tongue. Her soft fingers were playing with my balls, occasionally pressing and massaging, as it was her favourite toy in her hand.

The sensation of a warm and wet mouth sliding up and down was so intense. I was enjoying her every lick, tickle and suck on every part of my manhood and balls. I was drowning in pleasure. She started sucking and going deeper and deeper. I grabbed her head as she deep- throated. "O baby, go faster!" I growled. She was gagging and choking on my dick, but she was enjoying the feeling. She went faster and faster until my body convulsed as the orgasm hit me and I screamed, "Rachnaaa..." She was still holding it in her mouth as I unloaded.

"It was delicious!" She licked her lips and cleaned up my member.

We started our drive towards home as she finished cleaning up. We reached my apartment soon after.

My apartment was on the 15th floor, so we got into the lift. The moment it closed, I grabbed Rachna again and started kissing and caressing her. I pulled her up in my arms and took her inside the apartment. We didn't waste time in any formalities and went straight to my bedroom. We were kissing each other hard, lost in each other.

Suddenly Rachna pulled herself. "No, I can't do this to Rahul. This is wrong," she said breaking the spell.

I pulled her back in my arms and said, "No Rachna, what is wrong is leaving you unsatisfied," and I kissed her again. She responded hesitantly and as my hands encircled her in my grip once again, I could feel her resolve break and she kissed me back with renewed vigour.

We slowly took off our clothes, undressing each other while we hungrily gobbled each other. She was standing in front of me resplendent in her lingerie. I took off her black lacy bra and now she was in her red thong, only.

"You are so beautiful," I said looking at her pink aroused nipples that were yearning for the touch of a man. I started sucking them one by one. During the course of exploring her boobs, I took off her panty as well and put one hand on her hot core, which was already wet. I then made her sit on the bed with her legs split wide open. She jumped when I grazed her sensitive nub. I touched her silken smooth clit with my one finger and slowly rubbed it. She moaned as sensual pleasure swept over her body. I continued rubbing her pink pearl slowly and then fast for a few minutes leaving her with chills. She clutched my shoulders and moaned again, her hot pools flooding on my finger. The inside of her grew worse, and she needed me inside her. I slipped my two fingers inside her and started pumping.

"Abhi! Deeper, please!" She whimpered. I pumped her with my three fingers and she was gasped in pleasure. "That feels so damn good man…" Suddenly her body stiffened and orgasm hit her hard; her juices flowed freely.

Now it was time for the main course, but I wanted to taste her once. I slid down her body kissing her navel on the way down south. I was poised on top of her flower, which was open wet and inviting. I tentatively licked it and felt her taste in my tongue. As she moaned in pleasure, I darted in and started sucking her, lapping up her recent discharge. She seemed to enjoy it, pressing my head forward inside her white thighs. I finished lapping up her juice and moved up, sliding against her body. I stopped on her big white boobs and kissed her areolas, playing with them for a while. I kissed her lips and took my dick and started rubbing outside and around Rachna's vagina. She now wanted it badly, but I backed out saying, "Rachna I am not interested in taking you like this. I want more."

She was at her peak and couldn't understand why I had stopped. So, she literally started begging me to make love to her. I knew she was craving me but I wanted something else.

I told her, "I want to take you from behind. Your soft round white rump always attracted me."

She said, "I am yours for the night and you can do whatever you want with me. But I really need that hard-big rod badly inside my deepest core."

I relented and sat on the bed. She came and pushed me down and then came over me, gently rocking and rubbing against me. She raised her arms, running her hands through her hair, and pushed out her chest as she pumped herself to paradise. I shivered beneath such heat. "So beautiful," I whispered.

Resting her hands on my chest, she squatted over me with her knees spread, giving me the view of my life. Her slow and fast bounces were putting me over the edge. Each slide was a taste of lustful heaven. Her body trembled and begged for more. More of me, more of our lovemaking, more of us. She pushed faster and our hips slid against each other, helped by our sweat soaked bodies. She arched her back and moaned as she pressed against me again and again. Each thrust was more desperate and demanding than the one before it. I moaned louder. Each push sent thrills through our bodies. Each penetrating stroke demanded and she yield to me, to our joined, lustful desire. The ache was too much.

"Oh god! Oh god..." Her screams filled the air and thrust faster. Our slow lovemaking turned to a demanding rut as we each tried to bring our course of action to climax. Feral thrust after feral thrust made my body quake with lust-filled tremors of a pleasure I couldn't have imagined and longed to know. She ached for and dreaded the fulfilment of my lustful passions. Each penetration brought me closer to sweet, sensual fulfilment.

"Oh yes. That's it. Yes! Faster." I was grunting. She leaned her head back and revealed in the tremors that wracked our body with the sensual vibrations. This continued as she moved up and down for quite a few minutes before my body exploded into a sweet, lustful orgasm and I came inside her. She also peaked at the same moment and with her whole-body shuddering in delight.

I saw that Rachna's face was a little tense as I wasn't wearing a condom. I said, "Rachna, don't worry I am clean. You can take an i-pill tomorrow morning. Don't worry about it."

That gave her some relief. We lay on the bed entwined in each other's arms while she gently stroked my organ and I played with her boobs. We were whispering sweet nothings into each other's ears, but I was soon ready for one more round. I asked her to get on all her four as I wanted to take her from behind.

She realized the promise she had made and got into the position without any resistance. I started applying lubricant to her anal hole to lube it up and to give me a comfortable passage. I was also massaging her buttocks, so that she would relax her muscles, making it easy for her, when I entered her. Once I was sure she was well lubricated, I slapped her white round ass lightly; leaving red marks on them. She moaned in delight as I did that. I knew she was ready now.

Rachna said, "I have never tried this before and I am a bit nervous about it. It seems to be a bit painful."

I assured her, "Don't worry, I have lubricated you well. Keep your muscles relaxed and enjoy it. You will love it after a while," while simultaneously massaging her rump and alternately spanking her lightly and in increasing intensity.

I knew that she was as ready she was going to be and the more I waited, the more tense she would become. I inserted my organ slowly and bit by bit into her first. She moaned out loudly in pain and I whispered, "Unclench Rachna. You need to relax."

As she relaxed a bit, I pushed inside her and entered completely into her ass which was very tight. I could feel her tight sheath encircle my length as I pushed through. She gasped in pleasure as my length penetrated her to her core.

My hands were massaging her butt, and she loosened up again, giving me space to bury my organ deeper into her butt. She could hear and feel my balls slapping her ass as I plunged deeper into her.

This was a feeling like never before. I held her heart-shaped ass in one hand, massaging and slapping it alternately, while my other hand snaked up to her shoulder. I held her by her shoulder and pulled her closer, burying myself even deeper. She moaned in a frenzy not caring to be quiet anymore. She then came again, once more for the night in a shower of orgasm.

I finished along with her, spurting my seed over her round mounds while fell on her lower back as well. I helped clean her up, and we went to my adjoining bathroom where we took a long and relaxing shower. After that, we laid in each other's arms throughout that night and talked about her personal life.

Rachna told me that Rahul only cared about himself and was very selfish, both in bed and otherwise. He would be more interested in achieving his own pleasure and then would fall asleep. Similarly, he was never there for her as a friend and confidante. Also, the other members of the team had started avoiding Rachna as she was in a relationship with the manager and they felt that she might report their comments back to Rahul. The overall morale in the office was low and Rachna was at a personal low point, which was why I knew Rachna would succumb to my advances.

Rachna said, "Everything has gone wrong since the day you left the company," as she stroked my chest playfully.

I said, "It went wrong long before darling. It all went wrong when Rahul joined our team. But that is all in the past. I really hope you will stay happy with Rahul."

"Yes, our upcoming marriage was the only thing I could look forward to. But now I have doubts about that as well. Should I break up with him?" Rachna asked.

I reassured her that Rahul was the man for her and asked her to continue with the marriage preparation. We fell asleep soon after in each other's arms.

Rachna woke up early the next morning and left in a hurry, so as to reach her flat before her roommate woke up. I spent the next hour languidly in bed, basking in the afterglow of a night spent making love to a passionate woman.

* * *

Rahul reached his cabin and switched on his laptop to find five new mails, three of them escalations from their clients and a stern email from his boss. When he had booted out his main competitor for the team leader's race, little did he know the position would bring more headaches than benefits. He then saw the last email; from an email ID he knew very well but was not expecting an email from. The subject line – Happy Anniversary for becoming the Team Lead. As he clicked on the email, he was hit by a sense of foreboding. The email had a video in it, which he clicked open. It was a video of a couple in a bedroom. His beautiful fiancée Rachna, kissing a man he knew and hated. He sat and watched with helplessness as they undressed and made love, the moans captured by hidden speakers and every moment captured by hidden high definition cameras. He saw Rachna gave in, to do things she never allowed him to do. He could hear her moan 'his' name as he pounded her from behind. He was totally numb at the betrayal and was heartbroken. He did not know what to do next. Suddenly, his mobile flashed and he could see the name "Rachna" flash on it as he stared at the screen helplessly.

* * *

When Rahul had joined our team a couple of years back, he was less experienced than me, but had a very negative impact on the team. Soon, cliques started forming in our small team of five and office politics started. While I had the hots for Rachna from a long time and she knew about my crush, I never forced myself on her. However, Rahul, with his

Greek god looks and slick-talking, soon swept her off her feet. While I was a bit upset by the same, I never thought Rahul had something planned especially for me.

The position of the Team Lead was open and traditionally it went to the senior-most team member. However, on the eve of the announcement Rahul had a meeting with the management, where he shared evidence of inappropriate behaviour with a female member of the team – Rachna. Not only was my promotion barred, but I was also thrown out of the company without a warning.

It took me a few months to get out of the pit of despair that I was in before. I started piecing everything together and gathering information. Rahul had used Rachna to create a false case against me. While Rachna was not the mastermind, she was complicit in her silence before the HR when I pleaded my innocence and went along with the charade created by Rahul.

I started working in a security and surveillance company owned by a friend. After all, no one else would hire me with false accusations against me. Soon I was doing well and was making all operational decisions. But in the dark corner of my mind, was the intent to take revenge on Rahul in a way it would hurt him the most.

I used my professional contacts and experience to find out about his relationship with Rachna. While on the surface all seemed fine, it was not so great inside. So, I planned my revenge and enacted it out with precision.

Meeting Rachna at the club was not a fluke, but a plan. She got a text from a phone number of a friend she knew well. Cloned with ease and used to trap her, asking to meet her for drinks at the club. I knew finding her in this vulnerable position, getting her drunk and seducing her would be easy. Bringing her home was the next part of the plan. I had rigged my bedroom with hidden cameras and mics which provided Rahul with the best view in the house.

It took me almost a year, but I had my revenge, on both. After all, revenge is a dish best served cold.

LOVE
IN
OFFICE

Rajat had been looking forward to this day! They had been unable to synchronize their schedules for over a month, but finally, today they had a chance to spend an evening alone.

Rajat and Sakshi met a couple of months ago at a seminar. He worked as the Business Head of an apparel manufacturing company and Sakshi happened to be a contracted designer with the same firm, who was asked to accompany Rajat to the seminar. Rajat had hit it off with her the very first time that they interacted and she too had been totally at ease with him, much to the chagrin of Rajat's male colleagues, who all were probably harbouring some hope of getting friendly with this bright young designer.

Rajat had a couple of official lunches with Sakshi at the seminar, and by the time the three days were over, he had developed quite a crush on her. She was five feet four inches, with long dark hair usually tied in a loose bun, and her typically traditional sense of dressing made her appear a little older than twenty-six years. She had nice curves at the right places, a pert but nicely proportionate bust-line, and her fitted salwar-kurtas highlighted her curvy body beautifully.

Rajat had felt a twitch in his crotch from the moment he laid eyes on Sakshi, but her almost nonchalant attitude and her conservative style of dressing led him to believe that she was unlikely to frolic with a thirty-one-year-old single colleague!

Rajat liked to flirt his way into a woman's good books, and then take it easy until he made up his mind that the woman was worth spending his time with. However, he was yet to find someone who could hold his heartstrings for long. He was like a perpetual womanizer, always looking for his next conquest. In the three days that he spent with a well above averagely intelligent Sakshi, Rajat realized that he had never been with anyone like her before, for a number of reasons.

Sakshi started working about four years ago and worked hard to find her way out of her lower middle-class home in Nagpur and shift to Mumbai to land this job. He had always gone for the urban types before. Secondly, she dressed very traditionally, without ever revealing much skin at all. This was a variation from his usual choice.

Their time at the seminar had resulted in some flirting, which raised, among other things, Rajat's hopes of actually dating her. But the hectic schedule of the seminar and the fact that there was no hotel accommodation, resulted in no further action whatsoever from his end.

For about six weeks now, they had been exchanging emails and text messages which were almost suggestive. They had even met twice for coffee in-between meetings, but, obviously, the chance of something intimate happening in such a public place was bound to be low.

Today was a different story, though. Rajat had invited Sakshi after work to his cabin for a cup of coffee, and to supposedly discuss some designs. "I hope that the 'designs' you are mentioning, Rajat, are not the ones that you have on me." Sakshi had said flirtatiously on the phone when they fixed up the time for today.

"You're the designer, Sakshi. I'll leave the designing to you," he laughed. "My forte is manufacturing, remember? Let me see what I can come up with during our time in my cabin!"

The pun was not lost on Sakshi, who smiled inwardly as she hung up the phone, all the time wondering what exactly was in this man's naughty mind! She had never even dreamt that she would be attracted to a colleague, but this charming and witty business head had used his physical and intellectual attributes to such an effect, that Sakshi actually caught herself imagining him while she lay awake in bed, almost every night since that seminar! His six-foot lean frame often ended up next to or on top of her in her thoughts, and she wondered what it would feel like to turn her fantasy into reality! She had only ever been with one man in her life before, once. The rest of the stuff had been just kissing and some light petting. Almost all of Sakshi's sexual encounters had happened here in her bed at night, with the thoughts between her ears, and her hand between her legs.

For their meeting, as usual, Sakshi had dressed traditionally. She had chosen to wear a white sleeveless salwar-kameez and had left her hair open. The darkness of her dark wavy hair was contrasting well with the fair skin of her arms. This was more than she typically showed and gave Rajat hope that maybe she was trying to look good for him. And indeed she looked good! Her nails were well manicured and her sparse make up was just adequate to bring that glow to her face. It was obvious she had given good thought to how she was going to look for him this evening.

"Great to see you again, Sakshi!" exclaimed Rajat as he got up to greet her and gave a peck on her cheek soon after she was shown into his cabin by his assistant. "Finally, we get some peace and privacy; those last couple of meetings had been so noisy! I barely got to speak with you properly."

She smiled back into his eyes and said, "Yep! Finally, I get to talk to Rajat Mehra one-on-one, in his own workspace! So tell me Rajat, what do I owe the pleasure of this meeting to?"

Straight down to business, he thought. Obviously, it didn't augur well for his plans. "Let's start with some coffee," he said with a smile. "Work can always follow, can't it?"

They indulged in some chit-chat while waiting for the coffee to arrive. Soon the talk drifted to more personal matters, and once again Rajat found himself opening up to this wonderful, bright woman more easily than he could have ever imagined. They spoke about how he got into the apparel business, and about his friends and passions, and before they knew it, the coffee cups were empty and an hour had passed. As the time neared 7.00 pm, Rajat soon realized that all staff on his floor had left, including his PA, and they hadn't even started to discuss business yet.

"So do you have a lot of women coming to your office in the late and lonely hours of the evening, Mr. Mehra?" she asked giving him a quick wink.

"No way! Not a lot – only those who are terribly interesting, and hot, to boot!"

"So, should I be taking that as a compliment, or should I be offended at the shameless insinuations of my senior colleague?" she asked with a coy smile.

"The very fact that you are asking me this question means that you haven't taken offence!" he grinned! "Actually, one of the reasons for wanting you here was to discuss your latest design for the necklace paired with the red ensemble for the Italian buyers. I seem to be having some trouble with the production," he said, quickly changing the topic and pulling open his desk drawer to find the chain.

"As you can see, Sakshi, the design you have submitted has the clasp at the back slightly lower than the rest of the design. And, when we tried the necklace on our model, the clasp was protruding out by about 2 millimeters, making it uncomfortable for the wearer. Here, take a look at this," he said, handing the necklace to her.

She was mildly disappointed that the topic had switched back to business. Somewhere inside, she too wanted Rajat to get closer, even if just in conversation. Maybe something more would follow. She couldn't get enough of this tall, bearded man, and shamelessly imagined him doing stuff to her every time she lay down on her bed. But for now, she took the necklace reluctantly, and smiled slightly as an idea occurred to her. She wanted desperately to know if Rajat thought about her the way she did about him, and she had the perfect plan to find out.

"Hmmmm," she said, pretending to scrutinize the fastening clasp with a great degree of concern. She flicked back her hair and started putting on the necklace. "Let me see if the sampling guys have messed up my design specs! You seem to be right; this does look uncomfortable. Let me put it on and see", she said, as she fumbled with the fastener behind her neck.

"Uffff", she said, in mock irritation.

"Here, let me help you with that," said Rajat as he rose and walked around the table up behind her.

Her plan worked. Rajat was pretty pleased too. This seemed like the perfect opportunity to get close to her. He bunched up and pushed aside her soft wavy open hair. The fragrance of her perfume rose up to his nostrils, and he smiled as he said, "Here, I'll get that for you!"

She felt a small shudder rising up her spine as his fingers touched her bare neck. She was sure he must have noticed it too. He purposely let his fingers linger on for a moment at the nape of her neck, enjoying the fragrance and the proximity as he bent over to fix the clasp.

"What's the other reason, Rajat?" she asked, her tone now changed from the carefree one that she used a few minutes ago.

"Huh?" he asked, wondering what she meant.

"You said 'one of the reasons' that you wanted me here was to discuss my design, Rajat. What's the other reason? Is there any other reason?"

She was right! He had said that. He laughed as he realized how his sub-conscious mind had wanted this to happen. He now understood that she wanted it too. And he kissed her on the back of her neck and said, "This! This was the other reason why I wanted you here. To myself. I hope you don't mind me doing that?"

She felt a tingle between her legs the second she felt his lips on her neck. She couldn't believe this was actually happening! Not wanting anything to go wrong with this moment, she swivelled around in her chair and let her lips lock with his. The shudder went all the way down her spine and to her toes, as his tongue parted her lips and entered her mouth authoritatively. This man had her horny in a matter of seconds, and she knew that this could only go one way from here.

Rajat's heart was pumping furiously into his stream, a lot of it being diverted into his now slowly engorging manhood. As Sakshi opened up her mouth for his tongue, she quickly got up from her chair to wrap her arms round his neck, still lip-locked and breathing hard.

He wrapped his arms around her slender frame and pressed his crotch against her body as his manhood formed a big bulge in his trousers. Her urgency only made him hornier, and he started running his palms seductively over her back as they continued kissing.

"Ohhh, Rajat," she said, unlocking her lips from his. "I can't believe this is happening. I was so attracted to you during that seminar, but I never thought you would actually ... you know… being my colleague and all…?"

"Shhhhhh Sakshi. Don't talk! I want to touch you more. Feel you more. Kiss me, now!" He commanded.

Sakshi was even more turned on by the tone of his voice. She fell closer into his arms and kissed him deeply, while he pulled down the zipper of her kurta from behind. She hesitated for a second, once again, having mild doubts about screwing around with a colleague, but succumbed in a few seconds when she felt the heat of his palm on her bare back. His other hand cupped her breast over her kurta, and she was surprised at how quickly he had gone to her boobs. She was getting more aroused by his touch. She was scared, but yet excited at the same time. She wanted this, but yet, not. The time for thinking, though, was gone. He was already squeezing her breast, and the sensations were sending tingles into her pussy! She could now feel the wetness between her legs. The fact that his hard penis was pressing through the multiple layers of fabric wasn't helping. She needed more. And she felt shameless that she did.

Rajat was now pressing his crotch even deeper into her, kneading her soft breast, and exploring her naked back at the same time. He needed to touch her more – more of her bare body! He pulled out his hand from inside her kurta and reached under the hemline to pull it over her head. She was too shell-shocked and horny to object, and she stared into his eyes as he sized her up, the hunger clearly writ on his face as she stood in her salwar and bra. He stepped in closer to her, his hot breath millimeters away from her forehead, as he reached behind and unhooked her bra and helped her off it.

He stepped back and stared at her bare breasts with her large areole. She was embarrassed to be half naked in front of a colleague, but she was so turned on by the sheer audacity of this guy, that she stood there and stared back at him. She was getting so horny now that her juices had dripped through her panties and were starting to form a small patch on her salwar!

"Touch yourself!" Rajat commanded shamelessly, nodding his head towards her breasts. No one had ever spoken to her that way before. Her jaw almost dropped open at his tone, but her curiosity made her want to see where this would go. It excited her to no end. She reached up with her right palm and gently cupped her breast.

"Feel yourself! Not lightly. Caress your breasts. Tweak your nipples! I want to see them hard!" said Rajat as he started unbuttoning his shirt.

She brought up her second hand to her left breast, started caressing herself with both palms, and a soft moan escaped her mouth "Umhhh", as she simultaneously pinched both her nipples between her thumbs and forefingers!

Her moan made him smile, as he pulled his shirt out of his trousers and threw it across on his desk. The tent that his erect cock was making was now very visible through his trousers. And this excited Sakshi even more. As she felt a trickle run down her thighs, she wondered how wet she could possibly get! She continued to pinch her nipples and spread her legs slightly to get her balance as she started feeling weak in the knees.

He continued to disrobe – his belt followed by his shoes, and his trousers next. Within seconds, his socks, and boxers were in a heap around his legs, and he stood there stark naked, in his office, his cock exactly 90 degrees from his body, thick, purple, the veins popping up proudly through the thin skin of his cock, set against the dark backdrop of his pubes.

Sakshi had only ever been with one man before, in the dark of a seedy motel room 2 years ago, and had never seen a cock up close and so damn personal, in such bright light! The sheer girth of his manhood took her breath away, and she wondered how she would feel if he decided to stuff his 7 inch dick right down her throat. She was being commanded by this gorgeous stud, and she wanted to do his bidding badly!

Rajat touched the tip of his cock and got some pre-cum on his forefinger. He then brought it up to her mouth, and she stuck her tongue out and licked it as he stared into Sakshi's eyes.

"Untie your salwar and drop it!" he ordered Sakshi.

She was now too horny not to comply. Even if he told her to shove three fingers up her pussy, she'd only be too glad to do it. She dropped her salwar to her feet and stepped out of them. The wet patch on her baby pink cotton panties was plain to see! She saw Rajat looking hungrily at her crotch, and that only caused her to leak some more!

"You're a horny naughty girl, aren't you?" asked Rajat rhetorically as he slowly stroked his hard cock. "Get those panties off! I want to see just how wet your pussy is!"

His dirty talk was driving her insane. She almost ripped her panties off and spread her legs to offer him a better view of her now drenched cunt!

"Plant your naked ass on the table, Sakshi. And then spread your legs. This standing position – I can't see anything like this."

She walked up to his desk and propped her ass on it. She wanted to please this man. She wanted to do anything for him. She lay back on the desk, brought her feet up on to the edge of the desk, and slowly spread her legs apart. Her eyes were now shut in pleasure, and her breath was rapid in anticipation of what was about to happen. She couldn't help herself as her right hand went between her parted legs and she started to feel the wetness of her pussy which had now spread all over her pubic hair.

"Nice!" he said. "I like nothing better than a wet horny pussy. I bet you like to play with your pussy a lot. With a body like yours, I'm sure you have a lot of men lusting after you. Do you think of those men when you play with yourself Sakshi?"

"Umhh," moaned Sakshi in response to his question.

"Answer me!"

"Yes. Yes, I do. Some… some men. Unh … sometimes." She hesitated, "most times, I – er – I … think of you."

She had barely completed that statement when she realized that Rajat had quietly walked up close to her and brought his dick right up between her legs. She gasped in surprise and opened her eyes to see him standing between her legs, staring down at her wet pussy.

He had thought about this woman's body for weeks now, and finally he was going to find a way into her warm wet hole. Rajat's cock was throbbing as he guided the bulbous head of his engorged shaft towards her cunt. He made her moan as he first rubbed the tip of his dick against her wet pubic hair and her fingers. He then brought her fingers downward toward her pussy until she was touching her clit.

"I like that wet clit! Rub it for me, babe!" he said. "Go on."

And she complied. A long weep of pleasure escaped her lips, and she slowly started building up a rhythm while rubbing her clit. He was desperate to fuck this hot naked woman lying open in front of him. He kept stroking his leaking cock while he watched this spectacle, her hips now bucking up and down in anticipation of a thrashing orgasm.

Suddenly, he caught her hand and stopped her from rubbing any further!

"No! Please. Pleeeeaaase…," she shouted.

But he had her hand trapped, her forefinger on her clit.

"Keep it there. Don't move." He said.

He took away his hand and guided his thick purple dick-head towards the folds of her moist vulva. She moaned in pleasure at first contact and lifted her ass off the desk to help him gain better access. He slowly pushed his turgid cock into her pussy, and her warm juices flowed and flooded his cock as he entered her.

"Umhhhhhhh," he moaned as he tried to get some control over himself. He had to be careful, for he wanted to fuck this sexy girl in front of him good and proper before he blew his load!

The wetness of her pussy made it easy for him to slide in. Her mouth and eyes opened wider with each inch he penetrated, and her breath almost stopped in anticipation of the fucking that she was about to receive.

When he was all the way in, she closed her eyes and took a breath and laid her head back on the table.

"Now, start rubbing that erect clit of yours and with the other hand cup my balls and stroke them," he said.

She was like an eager beaver, pun intended, and complied with every instruction to the "T"!

She started moving her finger across her clit and cupped his balls with her left hand.

Meanwhile, he started pumping her with slow, long, deliberate strokes. He could feel the hot and sticky juices lining his cock all the way to the base. And the feel of her hot palm caressing his balls was driving him wild.

He upped the rhythm of his fucking, as his strokes stayed long, but increased in speed. She was now letting out almost a continuous high-pitched moan, stopping only to catch her breath enough to go at it again. She was rubbing her clit furiously now and her small little titties were bouncing in perfect circles across her chest as he established a good fuck-rhythm, and Rajat knew she was getting pretty close to the point of no return.

Rajat brought the fingers of his right hand and coated them with her slimy juices around his cock every time that he drew out after a stroke.

The index finger nicely lubricated, he reached under his cock and started working his way towards her asshole.

"UMHHHHHHHH!!!!!" she whimpered loudly when she realized where his finger was going. "Yes, fuck yes!! Do it!" she begged. Please, do it now!"

That's all Rajat needed to hear. He realized the second he touched her puckered hole that he needn't have lubricated his finger after all. This chick was so horny that her juices had traveled southward all the way to heaven! He slowly inserted his finger into her asshole, and she screamed, "OH MY FUCKIN GOD!!!!" and came gushing all over his dick without warning. Rajat kept his finger planted deep into her ass while ramming into her cumming pussy amidst her horny screams!

The heat of it all was too much for his sensitive dick, and Rajat couldn't hold on any more, and came gushing inside her. He sent thick long wad after wad of his seed deep into her pulsating cunt! He then pulled out his finger from her slimy asshole and stuffed it into his mouth, and sucked the slime coated finger as he kept cumming inside her love-hole!

They were at it, humping, pumping, wildly groaning, grunting and moaning for another few seconds, which seemed to last an eternity, after which Rajat pulled his now clean finger out of his mouth and collapsed over her naked sweaty breasts!

"You are SO fuckin hot!!!" she said rather uncharacteristically, as she shuddered from the after-effects of her orgasm. "Whatever gave you the idea of putting your finger up my asshole?? That felt sensational!"

Rajat stared into her eyes and said, "You've felt my finger there. How would you like to feel my tongue in your butt-hole?"

His dirty talk made her tingle all over again. "Oh Rajat," she said, "I've never ever had anyone talk to me this way, leave alone do that! I... I... don't know what to say to you! I suppose, umm, it is a bit late.

Maybe I should go now." She said, feeling self-conscious as their naked bodies lay entwined on his desk.

He smiled at her warmly as he rose from top of her body. "I suppose that is a good idea. I haven't even locked my office door," he said laughingly. "Maybe it's time we got dressed before someone walked in. But I have to tell you this – that was the hottest sex I have had in a very long time. A day into the conference, and I was imagining how you would look naked under my body!"

She laughed and confessed blushingly, "I suppose I have been thinking of you too, almost every single night. I just never thought I'd have the guts to go through with my fantasies! "

"Was that the extent of your fantasies?" he teased. And she laughed, leaving that unanswered.

There was a moment of awkward silence as they both got dressed. Rajat was the 1st to say, "So, where do you live? Can I give you a ride home?"

She hesitated before saying, "I would love that Rajat, but I think it will be out of the way for you. I live in Vashi, and you're only going till Andheri. You'll probably get home too late if you drop me."

"That's no problem, Sakshi. I'd love the extra time with you. There's no one to get home to, anyway. The family is out of town." he said.

Sakshi gave it a minute's thought and conceded. She had a great time with this hunk. And the extra time would only give her a chance to know him better. Who knows what the future had in store for her, she thought.

They managed to get into the elevator and into the parking lot pretty much un-noticed by the prying eyes of the office staff, any of whom would love to manufacture a nice scandal, seeing the senior business head leaving his office with an attractive woman at that late an hour.

As always, the conversation flowed smoothly on their drive. The lights and bustle of the city roads gave way to more desolate roads and darkness of the outskirts as almost an hour passed.

"Have you realized how easy conversation between us is?" Rajat asked her.

"Yeah!" she smiled. "I have realized, because it's rare for me to be so relaxed with a male. Most of the men I have interacted with invariably have a sexual edge to their talks. Actually, maybe you did too, now that I think of it. But, I guess, the fact that I was so attracted to you makes it ok!"

"So what did you think of me? You side-stepped my question about your fantasies at the office, you know!" He said with a naughty twinkle in his eye.

If his eyes weren't on the road, he would have noticed her blushing. "I didn't like you sexually at first." She confessed. "I was so impressed by the way you spoke, your humour and your wit, that I found myself thinking about you a lot. It soon dawned upon me how good-looking you are... and," she paused, "your beard... " she trailed off.

"What about it?" he asked.

"Well, that … was, um, one of the main things in my fantasy!"

"Really?" asked Rajat. "Do tell me more!"

"I guess I wanted to feel it. All over me." She said vaguely.

"All over?" he probed, purposely. Wanting her to say what he wanted to hear.

She blushed again. "Yes. All over. I, um... this is so awkward. You'll probably think of me as a prude. But, um, I have never actually had a man go down on me before. And, I wondered, how your beard would feel, you know, down there!"

Hearing these horny thoughts come out this normally restrained mouth was a massive turn on for Rajat. Immediately, he felt his cock start to harden again. "What else did you think of?" he asked.

"I wanted to go down on you while you went down on me." She said, slowly.

"You mean 69. You wondered how it would feel to have my cock stuffing your face while I ate you out, right?"

There was a sharp intake of her breath as she paused, and then replied, "Yes."

"Do you have any idea what these ideas of yours are doing to me?" Rajat asked her.

"No, what?" she asked as she turned her head towards him while he continued driving.

In answer, he reached across the seat to her thigh where her right hand was resting, and took it and placed it on his rapidly stiffening member.

"Oh!" she gasped as she felt his cock beneath her fingers. She pressed on the hardening hot flesh, and it sprung to life even more.

"Oh Rajat. You're getting all hard again!" she gushed as she closed her eyes and enjoyed the feel of his dick responding to her touch.

"I'm sure you must be excited too. You got pretty wet in my office!"

"Oh, I'm getting there again!"

"I bet you are!" he said, his eyes still on the road, but keeping the concentration going getting tougher by the second. The warmth of her palm through his pants was driving him crazy, and he wanted more. He slowed down, shifted the car in neutral, yanked off his belt and pulled down his pants while raising his ass off the seat.

"Help me off with my undies, would you?" he told her.

She promptly leaned over and got her left hand across his briefs from the far side, and put her right thumb into his waistband, and started yanking his boxers off. He helped her by raising his ass off the seat so that she could manage. But that action got his tent-pole closer to her face, and when she pulled the waistband over his engorged prick, it reared up and slapped her in the face.

"Fuck..." she exclaimed as she felt the heat from his cock on her face, and jumped back, causing him to swerve the car dangerously.

He laughed out loud at her surprise. "What? Too big for you to handle?"

"No way!" she exclaimed, getting hornier at the sight of that dick within eating distance. "I've been wanting to do this for weeks!"

The last words of her statement were muffled as she wrapped her mouth around his shaft and took him as deep as she could while moaning around his dick. She was horny as hell. And she was thoroughly enjoying the thrill of distracting him as he drove. Rajat would have liked nothing more than for this to go on for another hour. But they were just about 5 minutes away from where she lived, and 5 more minutes of this woman's wet mouth around his dick would make him shoot his load, and he didn't want that, quite yet, anyway.

Sakshi bobbed her head up to about 2 inches away from his cock, and stared hungrily at it as she aimed and spat 2 generous loads of saliva right onto the little hole atop Rajat's engorged penis, which was already oozing small quantities of pre-cum for the 2nd time that day. She moaned again as she deep throated him, and kept withdrawing upwards after each deep sucking stroke, until she had rivulets of her saliva all the way to her mouth each time she did that.

All this was driving Rajat nuts, and it was getting increasingly difficult for him to drive. He reached across from over her bent torso and tried to find a way between her legs. He needed to feel that wet pussy, and he knew it was going to be increasingly difficult to multi-task in this fashion.

It was now pretty dark outside, and the fact that they were far away from the main city meant even fewer street lights. Taking advantage of that, he slipped into a by-lane off the highway, and picked a dark spot to park the car. It wasn't desolate, every few seconds brought the light of some truck or the other across the windscreen, but both of them were way too horny to care about the chances of being spotted.

As soon as he switched the car off, he reached across and inclined her seat to the maximum. Sakshi was still bent over and sucking his cock hungrily!

"My turn!" he said in a raspy horny voice, as he gently pushed her back, more saliva strands formed between her mouth and his cock, and laid her almost prostrate on the passenger seat. He looked at her for a few seconds, hungrily taking in the sight of her heaving bosom. He wanted to taste her, and he was going to waste no time in being the first man to ever pleasure her by eating her out!

Rajat reached under her kurta and undid the string that tied her salwar. He used his right hand to gently lift her ass off the seat and pulled off her panties along with the salwar and yanked them over her ankles.

The musty smell, partly from the sex that they had had in the office, and partly from the fresh wetness that had formed between her legs overwhelmed him as he spread her legs even further.

"I have never..." she said hesitatingly. "No one has ever kissed me there, Rajat."

"I don't intend to just kiss you baby," he said as he bent closer towards her waiting pussy. "I will kiss, suck, lick, eat and devour you. You fantasized about my beard, didn't you? I want you to feel my beard graze against your inner thighs as I lick you to heaven!"

"Ohhhhhhhhh!" Her breath escaped her lips in anticipation of what was about to come.

Rajat bent over further between her spread legs, and licked her clit. She shuddered at his touch, which only encouraged him. He grazed his bearded cheek against one inner thigh, and then the next, and then flicked his tongue across her engorged clit, and at the same time moved his finger lazily over her labia. She jerked up in response. Obviously, this woman had never had a mouth anywhere near her pussy, and Rajat wondered how long it would be before he had her squirting her love juices into his eager mouth.

Rajat ran his tongue along where his finger had been. More bucking of the hips. And this time, a long moan too from Sakshi – "Umnhhhhhhhhhhhhhhhh, oh God, Rajat, yes! More. Lick me more, please!"

He was dying to taste her juices, and started rubbing the flat of his tongue all the way across the front of her pussy, sucking furiously at the same time, lapping up as much of her wetness as possible. She was getting so wet, that he couldn't even handle the quantity she was dishing out, and the over-spill from his tongue dripped down his chin and towards her asshole. Rajat didn't want to lose any of her precious nectars! He started making his way down towards her butt-hole, licking furiously all the way. It was difficult to gain access from side on in the front seat of his car, but he used his thumbs to spread her puckered asshole apart. This was it! He was going to ream this babe. He had to!

He saw the glistening cunt juice entering her asshole, and he knew he had to get a taste of that cocktail. She stiffened and stopped breathing at the touch of his tongue on her asshole. But when the tongue went in another couple of millimeters, she let loose another flood of juices flowing from her pussy! "What are you DOING to me????" she begged, excited as hell!

Rajat continued to shove his tongue into her, enjoying the taste and the texture of dirty insides of her puckered asshole and the juices all mingling together. Her ass was off the seat now, and she was giving him as much access as possible while willingly pushing his face down with her palm, even further into her asshole. After a couple of minutes of salty sweet juices flooding his open mouth and her asshole, he moved his attention back towards the source of the juicy river – her hot pussy!

Sakshi's volume rose a few decibels, and she started pushing her crotch upwards into his face, willing him to lap up more of her wet cunt. "Oh my god oh my god oh my god, was all she could incessantly repeat as the sensations of an impending orgasm started to overwhelm her!

The slimy pink open cunt was turning him on ever more, and he was like a thirsty dog between her legs, making animal sounds and shoving his tongue, nose, and as much of his face as possible, as deep as possible into her pussy. The moment the tip of his nose stimulated her erect clit, it took Sakshi over the edge, and she SCREAMED out loud as convulsions gripped her entire body!

She squeezed Rajat's face between her legs and she shuddered to an orgasm. His face was trapped, but that didn't stop him from furiously penetrating her insides with his now sore tongue, which only sent her over the brink further and into the throes of another earth-shattering orgasm! She was squealing and moaning and thrashing her head about now, and the shuddering of the pussy kept on and on in Rajat's mouth, and she rolled over into orgasm number three!

This woman was multi-orgasming in Rajat's mouth, and all the pain and discomfort of a squeezed head and a tired tongue was not enough to make him want to stop. Finally, after a 4th and a 5th shuddering orgasm she shouted out, "Enough! Please! I cannot bear this! STOP!" and she relaxed the grip that her thighs had around Rajat's face.

Rajat got up from on top of her with a wet face smeared with her pussy juice, and smiled as he reclined his seat and laid back on it, his cock hard as a rock, and yearning for release. Right on cue, Sakshi sat upright on her seat, and leaned over his cock and started to deep throat him! She spit on his cock repeatedly until the warmth of the saliva and the insides of her mouth became one hot messy cocktail, she cupped his swollen balls, and bobbed her head up and down furiously as all the saliva flowed down over her palm and onto his balls. Even onto his asshole. It was one messy blow job, and Rajat loved every fucking second of it!

He knew he was very close to shooting his load straight into her hot and horny mouth, and was using every ounce of his self control to prolong this sensation for as long as possible! His efforts were all put to paid when she moved her wet hand away from his balls and moved the saliva coated index finger near his anus. He realized she was returning the favour he did to her in the office and gasped at the first touch of a finger on his virgin asshole! The little distraction probably helped him postpone his release for a little bit longer.

But she didn't stop there. The lubrication of the saliva was enough for her to poke the finger into his anus, and he moaned as his sphincter felt a novel sensation. He never thought he would enjoy this, but the finger making its way slowly into his ass was only heightening every sensation he was already experiencing with Sakshi's hot wet mouth bobbing up and down his cock, and by the time her finger had slipped half way into his butthole, he was raising his ass of the seat and his cock which was now going deeper into her throat, almost gagging her, was shooting the hardest, craziest, horniest load that he had ever shot in his life!!

The semen hitting the back of her throat only pumped her up further, and she was rough in pushing her finger even deeper up his hole! The saliva coating only aided the finger fucking effort, and he was cumming and being finger-fucked at the same time for the 1st time in his life!!

He couldn't get his eyes off her face as his cum dripped out of her loaded mouth and down her chin. And he was now arching his ass off the seat, enjoying what was definitely the longest orgasm he had ever had!!

It was another fifteen minutes before they were both fully dressed and cruising down the last five-minute leg of the journey back to Sakshi's house.

She bit her lower lip unwittingly and smiled as she said to him, "This has got to be the wildest ride I have ever been on!"

"Tell me about it! My cock is still throbbing from what you just did to me!" said Rajat. "I hope that we get a chance to meet again soon. Really soon!"

She laughed at the desperation in his voice as he said that. "Oh definitely! There's still so much more I want to discuss with you. I hope we get enough privacy to have a nice, long chat."

She got off the car, bent and leaned across the window and fingering the necklace that was still around her neck and said, "Thanks, for everything!" and turned around and walked away towards her house.

* * *

SINFUL
LOVE

"Jai, will you drop me off at the college today? I am getting late." Radhika requested as she placed hot, aromatic parathas and rajma curry in front of Jai.

"Aah, Radhika! I completely forgot to tell you that my cousin is coming today. I have an important meeting in the afternoon. I can't cancel it. So, maybe you can you skip your German class today and stay at home. I will try to come home early in the evening..." Jai said without looking away from his mobile screen.

"Who is coming? I have to submit my assignment today."

"My cousin got a job here after completing his Ph.D. from Australia. He will stay with us. After a week he will moved to his own apartment."

"Oh! Which cousin?"

"You don't know him. He couldn't come for our wedding as he was busy with his exams. He will reach around 2 p.m."

Jai finished his breakfast and left for work.

Radhika and Jai had got married around one year ago. They had an arranged marriage. A beauty with brain, Radhika was an ideal match for Jai as per his family. Handsome and rich NRI, Jai was an ideal match for their daughter, as per Radhika's parents. After completing his higher studies in Germany, Jai started working in Munich and settled there. Jai, a simple man with traditional values and culture, had always believed in arranged marriage. He agreed to marry a girl of his parent's choice even without meeting the girl. However, Radhika never wanted to play this gamble. But she had no choice at that time when her boyfriend of five years was still not sure about marrying her. She surrendered and agreed to her parents' decision. Theirs was a grand big fat wedding. After marriage, Radhika and Jai came to Munich. Jai was back to his office the very next day and Radhika would be home alone for the whole day. Jai would be busy with his office work, meetings, and business trips. Radhika decided to join a German language class to keep herself busy and to meet new friends. Jai supported her. Radhika was trying to be an ideal wife and Jai was also trying to be the best husband.

Radhika was lost in thought when the doorbell rang. She looked at the clock; it was around 1:15 p.m.

'It must be Jai's cousin,' she thought and rushed to the main door.

Radhika froze as she opened the door.

"Krish??" she could hardly mumble.

"Radhika, you??"

Radhika couldn't believe her eyes. Neither Krish could understand if he was dreaming, or it was for real.

Krish looked into her eyes. There was a deep ocean of restlessness and hopeless grief. Her pain was evident in the crease of her lovely brow and the down-curve of her full lips.

"Are you Jai's cousin?" she asked.

"Yes. Are you the one he got married to?"

Radhika didn't reply. Krish was quiet too. Moreover, he was a little shocked. He had never imagined that he would meet Radhika again, and that too, like this. Once inseparable lovers were now bound in a different relationship.

"Come on in!" she said softly. Krish followed her, silently.

He settled himself on the couch. Radhika headed towards the kitchen to get water for him. She was clueless, whether to greet him as an ex-lover or as his *bhabhi*. Krish and Radhika were in front of each other after three long years. His smile and eyes were the same even today. His big dark eyes were not ready to miss a single look of her, penetrating deep inside her heart.

"How are you?" he asked when she offered him water.

"I am good," she replied followed by a long pause.

"Are you still mad at me?" Krish tried to break the awkward silence that prevailed between them.

"Should I serve lunch for you?"

"Only if you agree to accompany."

"That is the guest room. I have already kept towel. You may rest while I prepare for your lunch." She said pointing towards a room.

Krish closed his eyes, took in a deep breath.

It was five years ago, on their first day of his college when Krish had seen her for the first time. She had a comely figure which was twine thin. Her curvilinear waist didn't surprise him as much as the bronze tint to her complexion. Her skin was shimmering like gold. Her virility-brown eyes set his heart a-thump. Her crescent shaped eyebrows inclined slightly as she saw him staring at her. Her languid eyelashes of velvet-black blinked once slowly, as if to invite him over. Her nougat-brown hair flowed over her hourglass shaped waist. Her raspberry red lips positively drooled with goodness. Oh! Those sugar honey-sweet lips, her elegant personality, all mesmerized him. When he came closer, he noticed her scrolled ears and satin soft skin of her neck. It was love at first sight.

A smile crept with the tease in his heart, wondering about the old days and time he had spent with Radhika. Now when he saw Radhika after such a long time, he felt something in his heart.

Radhika's voice brought his thoughts back to the present. "Lunch is ready."

"Radhika! Say something. I can't handle your silence anymore. Please Radhika!" Krish held her hand and almost pleaded.

She shivered at his touch.

"Krish, leave my hand." She tried to get out of his grip.

Krish held both her hands strongly. Radhika stepped back, but the wall blocked her way. Krish came closer.

"I won't, until you talk to me." His voice was deep.

"What do you want me to talk about? What do you want to know?" She screamed. She was breathing heavily. He could feel her warm breath on his face.

He looked into her eyes. "You know how much I have loved you. In fact, I love you unconditionally even today."

"Then why did you leave me alone and flew to Australia?" she half-complained, half-repented.

"Didn't I ask you to wait for me for two years? You know I had worked so hard for that scholarship and that was really important for my career. I asked you for only two years, Radhika."

"So why weren't you ready for an engagement before going to Australia? We would have married two years later. You asked for two years and I asked you only for a ring exchange as commitment."

"So, you married someone else?"

"Do you have any idea under what pressure I was living? You left India and were enjoying a new life in Australia. And I was left back here to handle the family and society, not ready to let me live peacefully. I still waited for you for another one year."

"Then you could have waited for one more year."

"That's why I always pleaded you for the commitment. I just asked for an official commitment from you. I was ready to wait for you for my whole life." Tears rolled down her cheeks as she said this.

"Are you happy now?" he asked.

"I am married."

"That's not the answer to my question."

"How does it make any difference?" Radhika could barely breathe.

"Radhika... It makes a difference. It makes a difference for me. You have no idea how much I love you. Even today."

Krish and Radhika were so close they could see their reflection in each other's eyes. They could feel the warmth of each other's breath. They close enough to feel the heartbeat of the other, close to feel the shivering of the other's lips. And then their lips met each other, forgetting the real world. She forgot that she was not Miss Radhika Mishra anymore. She was Mrs Radhika Sharma now. He forgot that the woman he was kissing passionately was his cousin's wife. The only thing they could remember was their passionate love.

His tongue explored the depths of her mouth, and danced over her tongue until she had no choice, but to surrender. Her arms wrapped around him and her body pressed close to his. Her tongue met his, and thrust and parried in a breathtaking little dance that made her incredibly excited. She was so familiar with his scent. His musky smell aroused her. After all, the magic of first love is something different, something that never dies.

Radhika wanted him now. It was a hunger she had never felt before with Jai. Krish was truly driving her crazy. All the pent-up emotions of years and lust were boiling inside her and wanted a release. She wanted him to make love to her, slowly, languorously.

Her breasts smashed against the tightness of his wide chest. His muscular body woke a response in her. His hands ran from the side of her face down to her neck. His fingers moved, leaving the sensual trails as he stroked her velvety skin and then moved lower, dropping along the blades of her shoulder.

Radhika caught a long slow breath as his mouth left hers, but she lost it again when his lips met her neck, her ears. His teeth nibbled gently at her skin, his hands pressed the upturned curves of her derriere into his pelvis, his hardness growing as she rubbed against it in a helpless and involuntary motion.

Her breath came in hard pants as his fingers undid her blouse to reveal that lacy bra beneath. His teeth met the bra, and he teased at her nipples through the fabric, leaving wet rings on it and her body clamoring for more.

Krish groaned into her ear, a soft and low moan that made her belly loose and her thighs shake. She was swimming in sensation, lost in a haze of desire so strong that all she could do was hold on to him as he continued to touch her.

He walked her into the room and over to the bed and she went with him, their limbs tangling in their haste. Krish hissed in a breath when he saw her hair falling over him. Her satin skin was bared to him inch by inch as he removed the rest of her clothing and he stared down at her. His dick twitched in response.

He bent his head to her breast, his tongue flickering across the pink aureole and her hardened nipples. The long pale blue veins that meandered across her flesh almost stopped his breath; they were gorgeous and delicate, just like the rest of her.

His tongue moved across her belly and she instinctively sucked in a breath, flattening her stomach even further. He nibbled at her navel, making her squirm and gasp. His fingers stroked the wet entryway to her tunnel, then he slid one finger inside of her.

She was tight, incredibly so. He closed his eyes, allowing himself to feel her snug walls and the slippery heated oils coming from within them coating his finger, before he added a second finger.

His tongue gently massaged the tender bud of her clit, making a cry break from her full lips and more juices ooze forth and onto his own lips. She was sweet and slightly salty, her moist inner folds releasing more fluid to lubricate his passage as he worked his fingers harder and faster, loosening her for his cock.

Radhika writhed and twisted below the torment of his hands and mouth. He was driving her insane. She wanted him inside of her, she wanted to feel him touching her, pressing into her. She wanted his body on top of hers, his weight pressing her body deeper into the mattress.

His fingers fumbled at the button and zipper of his slacks and he was gratified by the longing expression on her face as she fasted her eyes to that heavy and lengthy flesh. His veins ran across it, pulsing with rich blood, his head was swollen and turning purple.

Radhika whimpered as he crawled up onto the bed with her, his knees parting her own. Her fingers dug into his coal black hair, tugging his face to hers for a long deep kiss as his hand guided his swollen cock to her slippery entrance. He rubbed the head into the juices there, giving her no time to think. She cried out, arching her back in desperation.

Everything about her turned him on so much. Radhika grasped Krish by his shoulders and they both went tumbling over. For a brief moment she was straddling his face, and his tongue sought out her clit once more, taking her to even greater heights.

She walked on her knees, backing up until her hips were directly over his cock. For a moment she was worried he would find out what she was doing odd or wrong, but his grin and the hands on her hips told her she had nothing to fear.

Radhika lifted her ass higher. His dick pressed against the soaked walls at her opening and then she slid down on his length, impaling herself on his enormous rod.

Her sheath spread for him, allowing him a deeper penetration, though it still clung tightly to his penis. Her gasps of delight and small whimpers told him she had taken all she could, and still wanted more. Her eyes closed and her mouth hung agape, the tendons in her neck stood out and he almost came just looking at her.

Radhika was close to her own climax. He filled her so totally and yet she wanted, needed, more- with a frenzied ardor she would have never thought possible. Her walls squeezed and soaked his groin with sticky liquids. Her hips rose and fell, her breasts bounced and her ass cheeks jiggled as she rode him wildly, with abandon and without any thought.

Desire was the only thing she knew, that and the sensations of his hands on her waist, on her hips, his fingers occasionally tweaking and rubbing her clit just to add to her pleasure and the feel of him deep inside of her.

She could not wait any longer, her head fell back and a long cry escaped her as her walls clenched and opened around his pulsing flesh. Krish thrust upward, his feet digging into the mattress as he sought his own release.

His cock pounded and throbbed inside of her. Every squeeze of her walls made new tremors roar through him and with every one of his own aftershocks she came again.

Finally, she collapsed, her long hair swinging across his face as she fell on top of him. His hands pressed into her back, kneaded her shoulders and tenderly stroked her hair while she gasped for breath and tried to recover.

Krish cupped her chin in his hands and gazed into her eyes.

"What happened?"

"Nothing," he smiled, stroking her lips with his thumb. "Why are you so beautiful?"

She blushed. "I have been missing these lines from you since a long time."

"Did you miss me too?"

"A lot. Every day, every moment. But never expected to meet you like this."

He kissed her forehead gently, and she snuggled down beside him, relishing the way her body fit so well into the curve of his.

She wanted this to last forever, but she already knew that it could not. Krish was almost asleep when she slid out of bed. "Where are you going?"

She wanted to get back in the bed with him too. So she said, "Nowhere," and curled up and slept beside him, inhaling his manly aroma and warmth.

SINFUL
DESIRE

After Krish came back in her life, Radhika's life has changed a lot since then. She really hated it when her husband Jai dismissed her each time, she asked him if they could go out and, perhaps, have a date night every now and then. She needed affection, time and attention of the man she was married to and committed to sharing her life with. But for some reasons, his work, and his professional life achievements were more important. However, in order to distract herself from her loneliness, she had joined the college to learn the German language so that she could find a suitable job for herself soon. She was spending more time outside, exploring the city and volunteering for an NGO.

However, since Krish returned, he was around her most of the time. She was feeling thrilled to be wanted. She was feeling exhilarated and giddy with him. Every part, every nerve, of her body seem to be resonating with joy. Even though that was wrong, it was feeling so right. She was struggling to understand. The force was too powerful and overwhelming.

Once again, she started listening to all those love songs, dancing on the tunes anytime. Dressing up and doing all those things that she loved to do.

But soon the week was over and now was the time when Krish had to join his office in another city.

"Can't you stay for a few days more?" There was a pain in Radhika's voice as she was helping Krish in packing.

"I wish I could stay here forever. But you know that's not possible honey," Krish replied cupping her chin.

"I am already missing you." Radhika couldn't control her tears as they rolled down.

"Aah! Radhika … Don't do this baby." Krish pulled Radhika towards him and kissed her forehead before wrapping his arms around her. "We will soon figure out something to be together. Till then you have to…" Krish said while caressing her back that was giving her shivers.

"Mmmm…" She moaned, feeling the warmth of his muscular body.

* * *

Radhika got busy with her house and college life, but Krish had left an emptiness in her once again. But he was dominating in her head. She kept looking at her phone for his messages and fortunately, he never disappointed her. Though they texted each other every now and then and called whenever it is possible.

'*How was your day sweetheart?*' Radhika's mobile flashed with the message from Krish when she was coming out of the kitchen after doing the dishes.

'*It's been a long day.*' She typed back.

'*My baby is tired? Need a massage?*'

'*What more could I ask for.*' She replied

'*First, let me take my baby to her bed.*'

Radhika thought to check if Jai was sleeping. The light of her room was off and perhaps Jai was already in deep sleep as it was too late for him to be awake. She decided to rest in the other room for some time.

'*Your baby is already in bed with her back aching badly.*' She texted

'*Great baby, let me remove your top to give your back a good firm massage.*'

'*Ohh! Please take off my red top. But I hope you will stop at the top. ;)*' Radhika teased him.

'*You think I can stop at the top? Snapping off your bra as well baby and taking off slowly.*'

'Ohh baby, the feeling of your hands on my back is perfect.'

'I am starting with your lower waist. Feel my thumbs running along the edges of your spine, down your back, up your neck and into your hair. Placing my hand towards your collar and you bend your head forward. I am making you thoroughly forget yourself.'

'I am moaning with pleasure as I can feel your fingers and your breath on my neck and into my hair, as you bend my head forward. I can feel the cold breeze from the air conditioner brushing past me and my nipples are hard from wondering where your hands might visit next on my body.'

'Once I finish with your neck, I slide my hands down your sides to your waist, lingering for a moment then wrap around to your front and slowly inch my way up towards your breasts.'

'I cup them in my hands and squeeze tenderly, but hard enough to make you catch your breath. My index fingers roll over your nipples. Can you feel me playing with your nipples'?

'I can feel your hands on me as I close my eyes and take a deep breath. I am getting wet between my legs baby. I squirm a little, not wanting you to stop but also hoping your hand will travel down my waist towards my wetness.'

'My left hand makes its way down the front of your body, while the right lingers a little longer where it is. The left enters, middle finger first, in between your legs, sliding forward and back with a subtle pulse.'

'I stop for a moment to remove my own clothes and then continue, making you wetter.'

'I love the feeling of your chest pressed against my back as you slide a second finger in, curl your fingertips slightly upward, and continue sliding them back and forth, making me more and more wet baby.'

'My right-hand caresses you down your side to your ass, continuing to massage you from behind. I bend you over further as I become aroused darling.'

'I lost myself in the feeling of your hardness against my back baby.'

'I am going to enter you now. I am pulling you back towards me with both hands, penetrating fully into your moist, inviting body.'

'I use the full weight of my body to massage you from the inside out, relieving the last, most stubborn of your stress.'

'I can feel your organ swelling inside me, feel the weight of your body against mine. I gasp loudly as I start to feel my muscles spasm against you each time you thrust deeper.'

'I keep pushing, until your legs quake and start to go limp. I hold you up against me and you start to sweat. Your heart beats rapidly and your breath gets heavy darling.'

'Baby I can feel your hardness going inside me deep. I can feel all the energy in my body concentrated between my legs. My muscles contract hard against your organ, bringing me to a state of ecstasy. Please don't stop, continue doing it harder.'

'Darling I am not going to stop. I continue pounding you hard and making you cum in relief. I can feel you touching the point of ecstasy and I continue at a similar fast pace.'

'And I collapse, spent as I discharge my wetness on your penis. And I smile as I feel your seed also erupt from your organ while you try to catch your breath.'

'Darling do you want me to clean you up now?

'No baby, let us stay like this in each other embrace for some time.'

There was no new message for the next few minutes. Krish was a little worried thinking why she stopped texting or did she really sleep off? On the other side, Radhika was feeling restless. She called Krish. He answered the call immediately.

"I want to see you, feel you and don't like to be so far from you," Radhika said to Krish.

"Neither me baby. I want to see you real soon."

Both gasped.

"Can't it happen that we are together all day and night at least for a few days?" Radhika asked.

"Nothing is impossible babes. Come over here. We will have a great time together." Krish suggested.

"You know darling, it is not that easy as well. Why don't you come here?"

"Hmm. I have a better option," Krish said.

"What's that?" Radhika asked.

"Let's plan for a trip. Three days in the Floating City of Europe."

"Are you kidding me? Are we planning for Venice for real? How do you know that it was always my dream destination?"

"Who else could know this?" He was right.

During college days, Radhika had mentioned this quite a few times.

Radhika was all excited, but confused at the same time. Should she go or not? What about Jai? What would she tell him if they really were to go on their trip?

"Radhika, I have to go on a business trip to Korea for a week. I got to handle a very important project. Hope you would be able to manage everything here alone for a few days." Jai announced at breakfast. That was the only time when Jai and Radhika actually talked.

"Oh wow. So glad that you got this important project. When are you leaving?" She asked.

"Next week. Wednesday."

"Three days to go." She calculated in her mind. "Perfect!" She whispered in the lowest voice.

"Did you say something?" Jai asked.

"Aah, nothing. I was just wondering what I would do here all alone. Even my college holidays start tomorrow and most of my friends are going on trips," Radhika said.

"You can also join your friends, or how about a solo trip?" Jai suggested.

Radhika knew that Jai would never ask her to go along with him. But to her surprise, he suggested she went on a trip of her own. She was even more delighted that now she could plan her trip with Krish during that time.

"That's a great idea. I haven't been anywhere outside Germany and India. I need to explore." She said with a smile on her face and glitters in her eyes.

She cleaned the table as soon Jai finished his breakfast and sent a message to Krish, *'Can we plan our trip for next week, anywhere between Thursday to Sunday?'*

'Yayy!! Seems someone had already planned something. Call you in some time.' Krish texted back.

Radhika was excited and a little nervous about her trip. There was not much time left for her shopping and packing for the trip. Krish had already booked their tickets.

She left for Venice on Friday morning. She went through the check-in, security, boarding and plane finally took off. The excitement of it all was finally catching up with her.

They landed at Venice Marco Polo Airport. Venice was a paradise. Long-awaited this trip was going to be more than just a bucket list destination visit. She had always dreamt to be in Venice for her honeymoon (that never happened). But she was glad that she was there finally, with Krish. The city was not less than a glorious charm.

They took a water taxi ride to reach the hotel. She leaned on Krish's shoulder. Krish wrapped her with his arm and they snuggled together. The sound of water lapping softly against the sides of the boat as they drift beneath iconic bridges and past its magnificent canal houses.

Radhika was so thrilled with the view of rippling canals, antique bridges and buildings were so fascinating. Everything was so romantic. Radhika was so startled by all of that. She couldn't help gazing in astonishment. She had never seen such a beautiful and floating city like this. The hotel where Krish had booked a room for them was indeed a splendour. It felt out of the world. It was beyond what it looked in the videos and pictures on the internet and magazines.

"Krish, I am going to freshen up. Would like to order something to eat in the meantime?" Radhika said to Krish as soon they entered their room.

"As you say." He smiled kissing her soft rosy lips.

Radhika went to the bathroom and quickly stripped to soak herself in a warm shower.

Krish heard the shower running and smiled at himself. He walked to the bathroom door and realized it was not locked. The door was cracked open, steam slowly filtering out of it. She was inside the glass shower cubicle, washing her long curls as the water and suds ran down her body. Krish felt his dick was already hard.

He pulled up his t-shirt, took off his pants and pulled down his boxers. Krish was fixated on Radhika's curves. He had caressed them many times, but looking at them now, purple from the warm water, drove him crazy. He slid the shower door open and stepped in behind her.

He placed his hands on hers and she slightly jumped.

"What are you doing?" She said in surprise.

"Enjoying shower with you." He removed her hands and started massaging her scalp.

"Only shower?" She moaned. "Damn baby, this feels so good." She tilted her head back as he let his thick fingers work.

"I know something else that will feel even better."

"And what that might be?" She turned around and looked at his dick. She rinsed the shampoo from her head and stepped back to him.

"I guess, you already know that." Krish pulled her towards him and tucked a curl behind her ear. Krish cupped her cheeks and moved her face close to his and kissed her pink lips. She flickered her eyelashes against his. The tiny wet hairs of eyelashes brushed against each other like the tender wings of butterflies flickering in harmony. He could feel the trembling sound of her heartbeat. Her body began to quiver uncontrollably. His head was angled slightly to the side as his lips came closer and closer to hers. The rhythm of her breath was in cacophony with that of his. Her warmth spread to him and he embraced her softly and passionately. Their tongue swirled around, exploring each other back and forth. Here they were, old lovers, sharing their intimate moments together. Their breathing became heavy and the desire was steaming.

He backed her against the glass wall and reached in-between their bodies. He dipped into her exposed neck and inhaled deeply, then kissed the base of her throat, tonguing her clavicle. He traced a slow circle on her bareback, driving her wild and she pressed her body against him. His touch sent seismic waves through her.

He noticed a few strands of her wet hair barely covering her nipples and carefully swiped it away, in awe of her form and sending a shiver down her back. A hot sensation travelled through her body as his lips and tongue moved down leaving the trail from her breast to stomach.

"Uhhhh..." A moan escaped her lips as he sucked and licked her wet skin.

"K- Krishhh." She whimpered as he moved his tongue to her womanhood. She squirmed in her spot when he licked her wet opening. The shower was hitting her breasts, gently fondling her nipples, until it rolled down her stomach and onto his forehead.

She pulled him up and their lips locked again. He slid one hand up her body and was kneading and squeezing her breasts, pulling, and tweaking her nipple. He let his two fingers inside her as his thumb stroked her clit. Her chest was heavy. He moved to take her other nipple in his mouth, sucking and teasing. He kept working his fingers in her wetness as she intensified the kiss.

"Aaah…. Krishhh." She gasped in pleasure as he broke away and pressed her body facing the glass. His body was crushing on her from behind. He reached around and slid his fingers again inside her, pulsing and pumping it. Glass was all steamed up with her hot breath.

Yes, yes…fast baby. I need more." She whimpered as he moved his fingers in and out faster. He was thrusting his hand with waves of water splashing over his arm enhancing all sounds. The water rolled over her clit, which was now throbbing for more. Hot juice flowed out of her body on his hand, spilling over her thighs.

Radhika turned to face Krish and they kissed as they did never before. She broke away and pushed him against the wall.

"Now it's your turn." She kissed him on his neck, trailed her tongue all the way down on his chest, stomach and lower abdomen until she got an eye level of his dick. She teased his balls and licked the tip of his hard manhood making him groan with pleasure. He let her mouth dominate him and he ached with the want.

She grabbed in her hand and started stroking it with while groping his ass with the other hand. She was licking and sucking the head of dick while rubbing the shaft causing him to tremble in her hand. She took it inside her mouth running her hot tongue all over his length. She was working with her mouth taking him deeper while inhaling his scent and exhaling. He started moaning as she stroked him. The warm water beating down on him was adding to the sensation with desire.

"Let me in you." Krish moaned and roughly pulled her up and pushed her back against the wall. She wrapped her legs around his torso and arms around his neck. Her pussy was ready willing to take Krish inside. He shoved himself inside her wet and tight sodden hole and started thrusting.

"Oh yes, yes…" She moaned as he reached deeper. He was thrusting with waves of water splashing over their naked body that was burning with the desire, enhancing all sounds.

He shoved his full shaft inside her, his balls slapping her clit over and over. She screamed as her orgasm set off like a volcanic explosion of intense pleasure. She had never known such absolute contentment, such intense pleasure, such joy.

"That was so amazing!" Both gasped and panted together. Krish smiled and kissed her before entering the room wrapped in a bathrobe. He wiped her dry, relishing each inch of her body. Radhika was getting excited but both were incredibly tired and sleepy. They decided to take a nap after lunch.

It was already evening when Krish woke up. He watched her sleep. Her lips were pinking and she was snoring softly. He chuckled and pulled the covers so that she won't catch a cold. He looked at her sleeping face again.

Radhika smiled as she could sense him watching her, even in her sleep. Or Krish was there next to her in her dreams too.

"You are blushing!" He said with mirth in his voice and she opened her eyes to her very naked man.

"Good evening," she said softly, still drinking in his masculine nakedness.

"And now you are staring," he said, and her face turned redder. "Don't blush." He teased.

"I don't have control over it," she said rubbing her fingers on his chest.

He chuckled and pulled her chin up and their eyes met. He kissed her lips and hugged her possessively. She could again feel his hardness. "This is what happens when you smile like this," he whispered huskily in her ears. She could feel the warm blood rushing all over her cheeks. She snuggled closer and kissed his neck.

He caressed her bareback under the blanket with his warm fingers. "Seems like you want me more," he said.

"Always!" She replied snuggling more into him. "Will you do me a favour?" She asked.

"Anything for you baby," he replied.

"Then close your eyes and keep your hands away. I mean don't touch me until my next instruction." She instructed. "Are you ready?"

Krish got excited listening to her plan and closed his eyes.

Radhika played a slow romantic song on her mobile and shifted her body sideways so she faced Krish, and slowly she inched her way over to him. His eyes remained closed, and she watched in awe as his chest rose with each breath he took in and collapsed at each one released. She rested her head on his shoulder and gently ran her fingers up and down his chest. She kissed his lips, he kissed her back. She brought her lips to his neck, and then brushed them up the side of his chiseled face, and up to his ear.

She kissed his bare shoulder blade down to his chest. His body tingled with excitement as Radhika explored his body with her wet tongue. She pressed her body against him, knocking away all his senses, making his nerves tingle. Krish was enjoying every bit of this slow motion. Every kiss and every touch of her soft hands on his rough skin was driving him crazy. Hardness jutted against her body.

Krish groaned when he felt her fingers grazing over his hot flesh, teasing him ever so slightly as his eyes rolled at the back of his head. It felt too good.

Radhika watched his face as she kissed and licked his inner thighs and played with his manhood. "Don't stop." He whispered.

His breath quickened its pace as she teased him even more, brushing her thumb over him. Krish moaned as she gave him a light squeeze. She was tongue teasing him all over his sensitive body.

"Can't have all this teasing anymore. Baby, I need to have you, now, please stop." he begged in his deep voice sounding raspy.

Krish pulled Radhika close to him. "Starter is over sweetheart. Now let us go for dinner," she said and kissed his cheek before leaving the bed.

"Let's first finish our main course here baby." He requested.

Radhika was already out of bed and put on her black off shoulder dress that barely covered her upper thighs. "You got to wait for that. Now get ready. I am hungry," she said.

Krish had no choice, but to follow her. They were walking on the streets near their hotel and found one quite restaurant at the end of the lane.

"Let's enjoy our dinner here?" She asked.

"Sure," he replied and led her to a small table inside. It was a late hour for dinner and most of the tables were empty. He pulled out her chair. He sat across from her. It was a cozy open roof restaurant. The only light in the restaurant was from a few well-placed candles.

Krish ordered red wine for them as she was looking at the menu. The waitress poured them wine and left the bottle to take the order.

"A plate of soup and pasta and a plate of fruits and cheese." Radhika ordered their first course.

Radhika blushed when she noticed him watching her sipping the wine. She realised Krish was looking at her for quite some time. A shy smile crept on her face. He loved watching her. He smiled warmly back. She was enjoying his gaze. Soaking it in. Feeling his eyes moving over her. From her eyes to her nose, cheeks, rosy lips. The curve of her neck. The slope of her shoulders. Her chest. The tiny bit of cleavage just peeking out from her dress. Again, she blushed. Their eyes locked across the table. Lost in the depths of each other's eyes. She could feel his desire. With a sense of longing to escape forever into that universe around them.

They barely noticed the waitress as she placed the first course. She gazed at him over her glass as she sipped her wine. She knew he was watching her. She slipped a grape between her lips and smiled coyly as her teeth crushed the skin, exploding the juices into her mouth. She reached for a strawberry. He deliberately snatched it just as her fingertip touched the ripened fruit. He grinned as he took a large bite. She offered her most convincing pout. He smiled affectionately and fed her the rest. Her eyes smiled back at him.

They continued. Refilling their wine glasses and eating slowly. Just enough to keep the wine from going to their heads. They did not speak, enjoying the company of each other. They ate slowly but heartily, sipping wine throughout; savouring the unique yet complementary flavours. They were eating in silence, feasting off each other's forks until hardly anything was left. Their meals devoured. Their appetites nearly satiated.

Dessert was served. A single dessert to share. A single spoon. He fed her a small bite. Creamy and rich. She could not help but smile with pleasure at the sweetness. Her innocent pleasure made its way across the tiny table, straight into his heart.

Then he took a large bite with the enthusiasm of a child. She laughed quietly at his playfulness. He gave another bite to her. Larger than the first. Some left on her lips. Of course, it was intentionally done. She knew it. He reached towards her before she could raise her napkin. He put his hand softly on her cheek and leaned toward her. She leaned toward him. And kissed her softly, tasting the sweetness of the dessert mixed with the sweetness of her. Everything around them faded away. They were in their universe, locked in a passionate kiss.

After the dinner, Radhika wished to take a walk under the moonlight and stargaze for some time. So, they headed off, with bottles of wine in their hands, following the trail of the stars. After a walk for around thirty minutes, they returned to their room and decided to spend some time on the balcony to enjoy the energy of the full moon. They were standing in the balcony under the full moonlight and facing the beautiful canal.

"You always loved this full moon night," Krish asked her.

"It feels so beautiful. I feel like I am so drawn to this moon as I am drawn to you," Radhika said resting her head on Krish's chest listening to his warm heartbeat and her hands held his right hand. Suddenly Krish started kissing on her shoulder and her neck. Radhika felt turned on by his burning kisses on her neck and shoulder under the moonlight.

"Krish..."

"And this was your fantasy to make love on full moon night. Wasn't it?" he said and pulled her closer to him. Radhika felt his shaft hardened.

"How do you know?"

"Ssshhh... No question. I want to make your fantasy happen now."

Suddenly, he lifted Radhika and she wrapped him by his neck and kissed him so passionately. He nibbled on her upper lip and she nibbled on his lower lip. They moaned, feeling the coldness of the breeze flowing. Krish pushed her against the wooden wall. Radhika moaned when he slid down her off-shoulder dress and started to suck her hardened nipple and was pinching the other nipple by his thumb and index fingers.

Radhika could not take it anymore and bit down his neck.

"Krish, please. Cannot have it more. Please take me now." She whimpered.

"Not yet baby. I need to taste you."

A few seconds later, Radhika couldn't take it anymore and pulled away from Krish and pushed him against the brick walls and smiled at him.

"Enjoy this!" She said and instructed him to sit down on the marble floor and Radhika placed her both knees on each side of him unzipping down his denim and grabbed his shaft member and placed it on her wet pussy clit and started riding him. Krish grabbed her round ass in his hands so tight letting out a moan like crazy and her breasts were bouncing on his face. Krish sucked the other side of her hardened nipple and moaned again. Radhika kept bouncing and pushing in and out and she had her head back and her hands on his shoulder, tightening it.

"That feels so good-aah! Krishhh...I am cumming..." Radhika moaned between words and her juices covered his manhood completely, keeping them well lubricated as it hit her g-spot. Her face suddenly fell in his neck, biting and sucking onto his skin.

Krish willed himself not to come just yet, holding back from reaching his release as she came around him, her pussy tightening around his cock. Her tight cunt squirting all over him had him shaking in pleasure, wanting to release all his juices inside her.

"Let's go inside the room," he said, and they stood up.

They walked to the bed and he put Radhika down on bed and quickly turned her to the side, moving behind her as he started fucking her from sideways. He raised her one leg up in the air, pushing himself deep inside her. He wanted to make her cum more than once, he wanted to make sure her 'under the full moon light sex' would be memorable. She could hardly hold her leg up, her chest heaving and she was out of breath. He continued entering her from behind, making the bed beneath them shake. He suddenly pushed himself out of her, guiding two of his fingers inside her tight pussy, only to make a cum-hither motion with them.

"You are so tight. Does it feel good?" He whispered into her ear. She desperately nodded against him.

He felt the uneven portion inside her, knowing that he was rubbing the right sweet spot as she grabbed onto the sheets tightly, reaching another orgasm that made her move her hips with his hand. While she continued to reach her high in waves, he instantly pushed himself back inside her pussy. Her mind couldn't focus on anything other than his persistent pounding.

Their orgasm collapsed together, and they gave each other passionate kisses making the purple mark witnessing their love.

He couldn't hold back anymore and released his juices.

"Oh Krish..."

The feeling of his warm juices hitting her womb and his throbbing penis shifting inside her made her orgasm once more. She moaned louder as her eyes rolled back.

Krish exited her body, both satisfied as they lay heaving on the bed. They were warmed enough to not feel cold as they hugged themselves close to another and he pushed the comforter over their sweaty bodies. Radhika let her eyes close and finally slipped into a deep slumber, Krish doing the same as he kept Radhika tightly wrapped in his hold, close to him.

* * *

Radhika was already dressing up when Krish woke up in the morning. She was wearing a white floral summer dress and looked gorgeous with her wet curls flowing around her shoulder. He smiled looking at her the way she was drying her wet hair. He walked behind her and hugged her.

"Good Morning!" he said, kissing her ear and neck.

His warm masculine touch sent a shiver to her spine. Butterflies were in a frenzy again. She blushed.

"You are looking gorgeous," he said.

"And you are so hot," she said, turning towards him, throwing her arms around his neck followed by a passionate kiss.

"Get ready soon. We are late for breakfast and we have lots of places to see today." Radhika pushed him to the bathroom.

"What have you planned to see today?" Radhika asked Krish while enjoying Asparagus Frittata for breakfast.

Krish was stunned and amazed by the beautiful scenic view of the city surrounded by sea and divided by canals. However, he was more interested in spending alone time with Radhika more than sightseeing. It was on the tip of his tongue to tell her that he just wanted to see her for the next few days.

"And now don't say you want to see me for the whole time," she said, before he could even reply.

"Damn man!" When did you learn to read mind?" Krish was surprised that how did she know what he was wishing for. Or was this what even Radhika wanted?

"So that was really going on in your mind?" She blushed.

They decided to roam around until evening and return to their room to chill and enjoy the last evening in Venice.

They walked across the elegant structure of Ponte Rialto, one of the two bridges crossing the Canal Grande.

"It is so beautiful!" Radhika swirled around looking at the beautiful view of the canal from the top of the bridge.

"Wait, let me click your gorgeous picture." Krish was capturing her delightful moments in the camera.

"Do you want to go for a Gondola ride or a walking tour?" Krish asked.

"Can't we do both?" She asked, pouting her lips.

"You know very well how to convince me." Krish smiled. "Let's go for a walking tour and explore the hidden gems of Venice and later we can return to the hotel by Gondola. What do you say?" He added.

"Sounds great as far you are with me." She agreed.

Krish and Radhika joined a Walking Tour group and were walking through a fascinating history of Venice. The tour guide was showing them a different side of the beautiful city, introducing them with the intricate details of the palazzo's, the elegant bridges, and grand churches.

It was already noon when they reached Piazza San Marco, the most famous square in Venice. The tour guide asked the group to take a lunch break. Radhika and Krish had a king-size breakfast late in the morning and there was not much space left for lunch. Radhika ordered a petty meal to share with Krish.

After lunch, they headed towards Basilica San Marco.

"Stunning!!" Radhika remarked.

"This is the crowning jewel of the Piazza San Marco." Their tour guide informed them. "This incredibly ornate cathedral was built in 1063."

The church was absolutely stunning with colourful details and glittering gold. The inside of the church was even more beautiful.

Walking through Castello neighbourhood was a fairytale experience as well. Radhika was soaked in the beauty of the city where around every corner lies another picturesque square, street, or canal.

* * *

After an early dinner, Radhika and Krish returned to their room. They were tired after a long day. Radhika flopped down on the couch and threw her feet up on the coffee table. She was feeling like she was going to sleep off.

"I am going for a quick bath. Would you like to join me?" Krish asked Radhika as he kicked off his shoes. Her smirk turned into a knowing smile as he lowered his jeans, revealing his rock hard cock.

"Give me a few minutes," Krish said and disappeared into the bathroom to prepare the bathtub.

He returned to the room shortly and started undressing Radhika. Radhika helped him to remove the remaining piece of cloth he had on his body.

Krish lifted her up in his arms and walked to the bathroom. Radhika entered the tub while Krish was at the edge of the tub. She lay back in the water, bubbles almost covering her entire body. There was a sexy gleam in his eye as he saw a shy smile on her lips.

"Scoot forward." He commanded. She hesitated a moment before lifting herself out of the water slightly and moving forward. Krish stepped into the tub and slowly lowered himself into the water. His legs were outside of hers, his dick brushing against her back. The warm water felt good to their aching muscles. But her soft skin felt better to him. His arms reached around Radhika and he pulled her back into him. Krish holds her, his arms around her waist, his lips on the back of her neck, her ass pressing against his dick.

"This is perfect. You look, feel, and smell amazing." Krish whispered in her ear, "How are you always so beautiful…" Krish could feel she was smiling.

His fingers began to dance on her skin, then across her stomach and sides, to right below her breasts, working down to the tops of her thighs. Her heart began to beat just a little fast. She spread her legs just a little wider. Krish knew exactly what she wanted, but he wanted to play a little.

His hands slid back up her body until they are both massaging her breasts. His lips found her neck as she rested her head back against his shoulder. He took her nipples in between his fingers and gave them a squeeze, raking his fingernails across the sensitive tips. Her breath caught and her hands reached for his thighs to steady herself. Krish was starting to get to her. He loved turning her on this much.

Radhika could feel his hard dick behind her, urgently pressing against her ass. Now she began grinding her ass into him. His hands momentarily stopped as he was caught in the pleasure of that sexy ass on his dick. But only for a moment. One of his free hands reached for her stomach, guiding her onto him further and harder. Radhika moaned. His other hand reached in between her thighs to tease the lips of her pussy. She threw her head back and opened her mouth wide as she finally was feeling his finger inside her.

The heat was radiating from both of them. Krish couldn't wait to get his dick in her.

"Lift up a little, baby." He commanded. Her hands returned to his thighs and she pushed herself up. She moved her hand to the edge of the tub and gently lifted her leg, sliding his underneath it. Then Krish does the same to other side and let her sit back down…right onto his hard dick, now trapped underneath her pussy.

Krish started pushing up, trying to tease her, trying to drive her insane but was doing the same to himself. She reached between her legs and took his cock in her hand. She squeezed him roughly and that was the last straw.

"I need you inside." She begged. Holding his cock straight up, she dropped herself onto him quickly. His hands moved to her hips to hold her in place. She began milking his dick with her pussy. His hands reached for her breasts again, leaving her free to control the pace.

She began slowly as she worked herself up and down his dick. His hands were massaging her tits and his lips nibbling on her shoulder. She was feeling his warm breath on her bare body. The wave of her desire for him was increasing. She picked up the pace.

"Harder, faster...keep going, baby." He groaned as he was enjoying the ride.

Her moans get louder, as her fingers dug into his thighs. An orgasm was about to hit. "I want you to cum." He whispered into her ear,

She grounded down on him one more time. She felt her pussy tighten around his dick and her body stiffened in his arms. The sound of their groan and moans filled the bathroom. She bounced harder letting out one last whimper as her entire body convulsed, she couldn't even breathe into ecstasy. Her hands had a death grip on his thighs.

She leaned back into his chest and he felt as she relaxed around him. Krish was still hard inside her. His lips found her ear. "Feel better, honey?" In reply, she squeezed his dick again with her pussy. "Radhikaaa…" he cried out her name. "I won't be able to hold it for more."

Radhika smiled wickedly as she lifted herself off him, onto her knees, and braced herself against the shower wall. She looked back at him impatiently, wondering what was taking him so long. Krish followed her gaze and went behind her, his hard dick in his hand. He rubbed it up and down her pussy, still trying to tease her. She was not in the mood to wait.

She reached underneath and took his dick in her hand. She guided it to her pussy and slid it in, just the head for then. She clamped down on him, knowing it would push him over the edge. Krish couldn't tease anymore. He thrust into her, hard, all the way. He needed to cum, thrusting her hard. Radhika was barely able to brace herself despite his grip on her waist. The water splashed around them as he drove in and out of her. "I am so close, baby… aah." She looked back at him with her wide and innocent eyes, almost begging him to stop. But her mouth was wide and naughty, demanding him go harder. He jerked for the last time with a groan, releasing his juice inside her. He collapsed back into the water, completely spent.

Radhika pulled him under the shower. They cleaned each other and wiped with the towel before entering the bedroom.

The entire thing was feeling like a dream. She could not believe that it was happening with her. She was just enjoying every bit of that moment. She was overwhelmed with joy by the whole experience.

"Radhika, I love you," he said as they lie next to each other wrapped up in a snuggly comforter.

"I know honey. I do too. Imagine having this for the rest of our lives."

"A marriage ruins everything, Radhika. Right now, all this is exciting, maybe it is because we cannot have each other when we want, that it is so intense. Marriage vows and bonds bring a restriction and a familiarity. Maybe we will get bored with each other if we spend just a few days together, who knows," Krish said and kissed on her nape before dozing off.

* * *

A funful and sinful trip of Radhika and Krish was over and they returned to their respective cities with the bagful of beautiful memories they created and lived in the last few days. Jai was already home when Radhika reached.

"How was your trip?" Jai asked. Hearing his voice, Radhika felt like someone woke her up to reality from a beautiful dream.

"It was good," She replied with a short smile. " How was yours?"

"It was successful. As usual, only work and work."

"Hmm...Agreed," she said with a nod.

It's been two weeks since Radhika came to Germany. Radhika and Jai were back to their old routine. Jai was again busy with office and work and Radhika engrossed herself with her studies and other college activities. Krish was connected to her over phone and video calls and whatsapp messages when anyone of them was busy.

One day when Jai was in his office, he got a call from Radhika. When he picked up the call, he found some other girl talking on the other side. She was Radhika's college friend and informed Jai about Radhika falling sick. Jai rushed to the college to pick her. Radhika had viral fever for the next few days. And these few days she was surprised to see a completely different Jai. He was a new Jai who has turned into a very caring husband. Although he was still not talking much, he was taking care of her in all possible ways. He was working from home to be around her. He was cooking special meals for her, giving her medicines, supporting her to walk if she felt weak or even he would carry her in his arms and make her sit on the sofa in the drawing room if she was getting bored of being in the bedroom for long.

Soon Radhika got well and started going to her college. Jai also joined his office. Things were normal again with a small change. Now Jai tried his best to spend more time with Radhika and Radhika also began to understand his silent gestures for her.

Her illness brought them closer. In these days Radhika started feeling for Jai. But a conflict began within her. Did she really love Krish or was it her loneliness that attracted her towards him? It was the gap between her and her husband and the emptiness in her life that Krish was just filling. And now when she was getting all attention, time, and care from her husband, Krish was nowhere on her mind. Slowly their number of chats and duration of calls reduced. Even Krish got busier in his own life or maybe he got someone in his office with whom he was weaving a new love story.

However, life is never a smooth ride. Something else was waiting to surprise her and to take her on a roller coaster ride of thoughts. She was shocked when she found out that she was pregnant. There was no doubt that the baby was Krish's. She did not tell Krish or her husband about her pregnancy yet.

She was only sure about having and keeping the baby. Aside from that, she was at a loss about what to do. Soon her baby bump would start to show. She guessed she would have to decide to tell Jai and Krish about it.

She was in a dilemma on what to do. Should she tell the truth to them or just hide it from Krish and seduce Jai and then make him believe that the baby was his. She certainly didn't need to complicate her life with an affair. She decided to work on the second option.

THE
CHALLENGE

My name is Rakesh Arora. I have been married for almost seven years and my wife Nisha was the perfect partner for me. She was beautiful, intelligent and sexy. We had met at an arranged set up and then gotten married. We had been together for seven years, but we still could not keep our hands off each other. I am a Corporate Lawyer by profession and a successful one at that. My law firm had grown from a two-man partnership to a twenty-person firm over the length of my marriage.

We would work hard and had some of the top Indian businesses and startups as our clients. With rising valuations, these clients worked hard over the week and partied harder over the weekend. There was once a party at one of the client's house on a Saturday evening. We went there as Ankit was well-known for his legendary house parties. He had a nice farmhouse outside the city and his poolside parties would be a total rave. His guest list had everyone from celebrities to politicians, from models to startup icons. Here, people let their hair down and went crazy, with alcohol flowing like water.

Nisha was looking hot, probably the hottest chic in the whole party. She was wearing a white dress with red lipstick and she had really sexy lingerie on below. Everyone was staring at her, even Ankit. We all laughed, ate together. Ankit even had hookah for us which we both smoked. It was quite well made and we both got high. I was sitting on the sofa and I saw Ankit with his hands around Nisha's waist on the balcony and they were both laughing, pretty close to each other.

Later Ankit came to me and said, "Dude, I wanna sleep with your wife".

I said, "I am sure you and everyone else in this party, but she won't let anyone but me touch her."

He said quite casually, "Are you sure?"

This was a challenge I could not reject, so I said, "I can bet you ten lakh rupees she won't." He agreed and went away. We came back home later in the night, and forgot about all that had happened at the party.

One week later, I got a package marked "Confidential" at the office. In my line of work as a lawyer, this wasn't unusual, but as I inspected the package, I noted that it had no return address.

Inside the packet, I found a USB drive and a piece of folded paper. Opening the paper, I discovered a handwritten note stating simply - "You owe me ten lakh."

I put the USB on my laptop and clicked the mouse on "Play". The video began by showing a large bedroom that I didn't recognize, until Ankit walked into the room ... leading my wife by her hand. I stopped the video and picked up the phone to call my secretary.

"Tina ... No calls, please." Hanging up, I clicked "Play" again.

After watching for a few moments, it became obvious that Ankit had at least five different cameras hooked up in his bedroom. The pictures and sound were crystal clear, the audio/video equipment must have been the top of the line from his chain of stores.

Nisha was wearing the dress I had seen her in last weekend, the same that she had worn the previous evening to the party. She had also applied the light brown eyeshadow with glitter and her lips glistened in a soft, red shade. Ankit was shirtless, wearing only a pair of long, baggy swimming trunks.

He led her over towards the large painting next to his bed, and then stood directly behind her, both holding tall champagne glasses.

"Oh Ankit!" my wife exclaimed. "It is beautiful. I love the colours that have been used. They are so vibrant... vivid really."

As she spoke, Ankit placed his hand softly on my wife's bare midsection, just above the gentle swell of her hip. I saw Nisha's eyes dart down to his hand when she felt his touch, but she did not move away or voice any objection. Instead, I could see a thin smile start to form on her lips.

Still standing behind her, Ankit slowly slid his hand across the front of her tight, tan tummy and down between her legs. Nisha spread her legs slightly as he began to gently rub her pussy on the outside of her suit. Her eyelids drooped, now leaning back into his broad shoulders.

With a groan, Nisha turned into his arms, her face inches from his. Looking up into his eyes, she said softly, "I really shouldn't be here."

Ankit took her glass from her hand and placed it on the bedside table with his own. He put both his hands on her hips, my wife responding by resting her hands lightly on his tanned and corded forearms.

"You are free to leave if you want," Ankit told her.

Nisha quickly responded with a sexy smile, "Oh no... You misunderstood me. I said I shouldn't be here. I didn't say anything about wanting to leave!"

With that, she lifted her arms up over his shoulders and pulled his face down to her hungry lips. They kissed softly at first, Nisha's tongue darting into his open mouth, before Ankit pulled her into his hot embrace. His lips pressed hard against hers, her hands sliding down to cradle the sides of his face as their tongues duelled. Ankit cupped one of my wife's firm breasts in his hand, his thumb lightly gliding across and already stiff nipples.

Nisha moaned softly into his mouth as they kissed passionately, his hands now on her tight ass cheeks, pulling her hard against his bulging crotch.

They continued to kiss for several minutes. My wife's hand slid into the waistband of his swimsuit, fondling his cock. Ankit pulled away from her luscious lips, leaving her panting. He took a step, a smug look on his face, and put his hands on Nisha's shoulders applying slight downward pressure. My wife, clearly recognizing what he wanted, eagerly got to her knees pulling his suit to his ankles with a firm tug.

Ankit's cock sprung free and Nisha quickly grabbed it, her eyes wide in a mixture of surprise and delight. He appeared to be really long, with a thick shaft that my wife's hand could not completely encircle. My wife brought his cock to her lips and lovingly kissed its bulbous head, her tongue snaking out to lick its tip. She dropped her jaw and took him into her mouth, slowly bobbing her head as she stroked him with both of her tiny hands.

Ankit started talking to her, "Oh... That's it! That feels good... But you gotta suck it harder... I like you to suck it real hard!!"

I saw my wife's cheeks hollow as she did as she was told, and you could hear her slurping and slobbering over his thick member. Ankit groaned loudly, clearly approving of her response. Nisha pulled her lips away with an audible pop and looked up at Ankit panting.

"Is that better?" she asked eagerly "Does that feel good, baby!?"

"Ahh... Shit! Ohh yeah! That's much better!" Ankit laughed in response. Nisha lowered her head, as she lifted his long cock upward, her tongue darting out to lightly lick his smooth sack.

"Aaahhhh... Nisha! That's it! Now... suck my balls! Put them in your mouth and suck...!"

Ankit's eyes closed, his head arched backward as my wife slurped, first one, then his other heavy nut past her wetly shining lips, sucking hard. She continued to stroke his hard shaft as she sucked him, the diamonds in her wedding bands sparkling in the bright sunlight that illuminated his bedroom.

Ankit spread his legs and continued to guide her "Now... I want you to lick right behind my balls!" My wife bent further, her head now between his legs. "Oh yeah... That's it... That's ... Oh shit!!"

After returning to sucking his balls, Nisha licked slowly up his hard shaft and took him back into her mouth, her head bobbing at a steady rhythm.

Ankit pushed her hair back from her face and whispered "Look at me, baby! I want to look at you with my cock in your mouth."

Nisha stopped and did as she was told, looking up at Ankit from her knees, a pleased smile on his face.

"Aaaah!... You are so beautiful!! I wanted you like this from the first minute I saw you! Do you like sucking my dick? Does it taste good?!"

My wife started to pull her head back to answer, but Ankit quickly stopped her.

"No... Don't move! Do you like sucking my cock?" he asked again in a firm tone.

Nisha's muffled response sounded like an enthusiastic "Mmmmmm Hhhhmmmmm!!!!!"

Ankit smiled. "That's better. I want to hear you while you suck me! I want you to show me how much you love it!"

Nisha began moaning loudly as she sucked him, her head now rapidly bobbing over his length. I couldn't believe he hadn't peaked yet.

Ankit pulled his wetly shining shaft from my wife's lips and held his cock away from her. When she reached for it with her open mouth, he pulled it further away.

"Wait!" he instructed. "Sit back. Now... Open your mouth. That's it! Stick your tongue a little bit!" Nisha did as she was told.

Ankit smacked his thick cock against her lips and tongue several times, occasionally also smacking her nose and cheeks.

Ankit suddenly slammed his cock back in my wife's mouth, his hands now holding her head as he started to drive faster. Nisha put her hands on his thick thigh muscles and tried to hang on as he continued to drive his long shaft into her mouth, groaning like a crazy man.

He stopped as abruptly as he had started and told Nisha to take off her top. Learning from her earlier mistake, she kept him in her mouth as she reached behind her back to untie the string, pulling the suit off her shoulders and casting it on the bedroom floor. She continued to blow him as Ankit peered down at her.

Nisha pushed her full, firm tits together as her mouth continued to hungrily work his cock, moaning as she did so. Ankit pulled his cock away with a pop and my wife looked up at him, still cupping her breasts, her face flushed, her eyes filled with lust.

Ankit ran his cock over her upraised boobs, her nipples swollen, my wife still kneeling in front of him clothed only in her tiny bikini bottom and high heels.

"I want to take you now," he said matter-of-factly. "I need you now. Get on the bed!"

My wife quickly got to her feet and walked towards the king-sized bed. She started to kick off her heels, but Ankit told her, "Leave those on." They make you look even hotter. I like that."

Nisha undid the side-ties, allowing the suit to fall to the floor, revealing a closely trimmed triangle above her moist slit.

"Lie down and spread your legs. That's it! Now... I want you to touch yourself! Show me how you touch yourself when you get excited!"

My wife reached between her legs and started to rub her pussy in a circular fashion, her hips grinding against her hand.

Nisha began to moan as she fingered her clit, Ankit grinning at the sight of my lovely wife working herself towards and orgasm.

"Are you wet? Lick your fingers... I want you to taste yourself. Am I gonna like your pussy?" he prodded.

Nisha daintily licked at her finger before plunging it into her mouth, sucking it clean.

"Oh god! I'm so wet... So hot. God, I want you so bad."

Ankit strode towards the bed, his erection bobbing proudly in front of him. He kneeled between my wife's outstretched legs and stroked his cock as she continued to finger her pussy.

"What do you want me to do, Nisha? Or should I say, Mrs. Khanna."

"Give me your big cock, baby! You have no idea how badly I need this," she pleaded with him.

"What about your husband?" he mocked as he leaned forward rubbing the head of his cock over her swollen pussy lips, causing her to shudder.

"Don't... Don't talk about him," Nisha moaned, clearly unsettled that he had mentioned me. "Just do me. Now! Don't tease me like this."

"But you're married. Are you sure you want to do this?"

Ankit pushed the bulbous head of his cock into her pussy, but quickly withdrew it.

"Ooohhh God! Please make love to me. I want you to take me, baby. Please... Just give me your big cock!" Nisha was squirming beneath his bulk. "Just make love to me, baby. I want... OOOOOHHHHH SSSHHIITTTTT!!!!!!"

Ankit caught my wife off guard as she was begging to be ravished, sliding his long, hard shaft deep inside her. She inhaled sharply as he began to slowly saw in and out of her, his ass cheeks flexing. My wife's head rolled on the bed, her hip driving off the mattress to meet her lover's thrusts, a smug smirk on his lips.

"You like me inside you?" he asked as he drove into her. "How does that feel?"

"Aaaaahhh... Yeahhh!... So good!... So... so good. Make love to me, baby!! Just keep loving me."

Ankit lowered his lips towards hers and my wife reached up to grab the sides of his face, thrusting her tongue deep into his mouth, as she ground her hips against him. The wet slap of their bodies mixing erotically with her moans and the creak of the bedsprings were echoing in my ears.

Ankit buried his cock to the hilt in my wife, his head arched back, his mouth open.

"Aaaahhh shit, baby!... You are so tight. You are so wet." He started moving more slowly, rolling at the bottom of his strong thrusts, my wife wriggling eagerly beneath him.

After grinding slowly against her for several minutes, Ankit raised himself up on his arms and picked up the pace of his thrusts, his hips driving furiously between my wife's outstretched legs. Nisha's hands grabbed his tight ass cheeks as he slammed into her, pulling him hard against her as she lifted her hips off the bed to meet his thrusts.

"Ooohh baby! Don't stop! You're gonna make me cum."

Ankit continued his assault, slamming his long, thick rod deep into my wife's pussy, her heavy breasts bouncing with each hard thrust.

When her orgasm hit, Nisha inhaled sharply before shouting, "OOOOOHHHHHH MMMMYYY GGAAWWDDD!!"

Her body shuddering beneath her young lover, her thighs noticeably twitching, her breathing shallow and ragged. She tossed her head back and forth on the bed and arched her back, her French-manicured nails biting into Ankit's ass cheeks as he continued to saw his cock into her depth.

"Aaahh... yeahh!... Oh god!... Oh my god! Oh ... OH ...OH!" she moaned as her orgasm coursed through her lithe body, her eyes screwed shut.

When she finally opened her eyes, she was panting like she had just run a marathon, a look of wonder on her face. Ankit looked down and smiled, his body continuing to slap against hers.

After she caught her breath, my wife reached up towards Ankit's face, pulling him down, her mouth open and her tongue extending to meet his. They kissed softly and Ankit settled between her legs, his cock bottomed out in her pussy.

When he finally pulled away from her hungry lips, Ankit started to pound his thick shaft in a deep, steady rhythm, building up his speed. Nisha sensed that he was working up to his own orgasm and ground her hips against him, urging him on in a slutty tone.

"That's it, baby. Give it to me! You are so big and it feels so good in my hot pussy."

Ankit picked up his pace, a pleased smile on his face. "OHHH... Shit!!... I'm gonna give it to you. I'm gonna cum... I wanna cum in your mouth. Let me cum in your mouth."

"Give it to me, baby!" my wife pleaded "I want to taste your cum! Give it to me."

Ankit groaned and continued to thrust inside Nisha for a few moments longer before pulling his wetly shining cock from between her legs and moving up quickly to straddle her face. Nisha raised her head and brought one arm under his legs to reach for his cock, bringing it to her lips. Taking him quickly into her mouth as she frantically stroked his shaft, Ankit threw his head back, tensing before he groaned and exhaled, his body jerking as he shot load after load of his hot cum into my wife's eager mouth. Nisha was moaning with lust as she struggled to swallow his seed, working his hard shaft with her hand.

With a final moan and involuntary shudder, Ankit's climax was over, his chest rising and falling. Nisha nevertheless continued to suck, only reluctantly relinquishing his now flaccid manhood when it slid from her lips. She planted a sloppy kiss on the mushroom head of his dick before Ankit rolled away.

Nisha looked at the man lying naked next to her with a questioning smile on her face. Ankit laughed when he caught her looking at him with big puppy dog eyes.

"What!" he sputtered, raising an arm so she could cozy up next to him, her head on his shoulder, her hand on his chest.

"Nothing!" she responded, a pleased and contented smile on her lips. She squeezed him tightly in her arms, kissing him on the chest.

When Ankit sat up against the headboard, Nisha did the same, fluffing a pillow behind her back. He reached inside the bedside table and pulled out his silver cigarette case. He lit one of his long, dark cigarettes and offered it to my wife. She took it between her outstretched fingers and brought it to her lips, taking a slow drag. She exhaled and watched as Ankit lit a cigarette for himself before settling back against the headboard. Ankit reached for his champagne glass and drained its contents before handing both their glasses to Nisha.

"How about you freshen these up? You made me thirsty!" he added with a sly grin.

Nisha grinned back and took the glasses from him. Moments later, she returned with their drinks and sat on Ankit's side of the bed, one slender leg bent and raised, lying against his muscular thigh.

As Ankit sipped from his glass, my wife took another drag on her cigarette and exhaled a thin stream away from the bed. Ankit looked at her with raw lust in her eyes.

"Damn... You are so gorgeous. So damn sexy! I wanted you so bad I could barely take my eyes off you at the party!"

Nisha laughed in response "I noticed!" I wasn't surprised at all when you called this morning."

"I gotta admit... I was a little surprised that you agreed to see me. Have you done this before?"

"Of course I've done this before... I've been married for seven years!" Nisha replied with a sly grin.

Initially confused, Ankit's eyes narrowed before he grinned and said, "No... I don't mean this..." he lifted his thick cock and pointed it my wife "I mean this!" picking up her hand and directing her attention to her wedding bands.

"I knew what you meant the first time!" Nisha teased "And the answer is 'no' I've never slept with anyone but my husband."

Ankit studied my wife closely to determine if she was joking with him again. "Really? Nothing at all? I can't believe that I'm your first lover."

My wife shrugged her shoulders and looked away briefly as she took a long drag from her cigarette. She then lowered her mouth to his cock, kissing and licking its bulbous head, before leaning over further, her mouth dancing slowly across his tight abs, before nibbling at the front of his cock.

With a low moan, my wife began to lustily suck her lover's cock, one hand working in unison with her loving mouth, the other cupping his heavy ball sack.

It was clear my wife was a quick study when it came to oral treats. Her cheeks hollowed as she sucked his thick shaft, moaning and slurping with the enthusiasm of a well-paid whore. She took each of his balls into her mouth and ran the tip of her tongue lightly up and down the front of his shaft, finally taking his cock back into her mouth. Ankit clenched his ass, clearly enjoying my wife's efforts.

She pulled her lips off with a loud pop and studied his wetly shining manhood. Smiling sexily at Ankit, my wife rolled over onto her back and spread her legs, one hand sliding across her flat tummy to her pussy where she began to rub her swollen clit.

Ankit quickly knelt between her legs and eased the thick head of his straining cock past my wife's pussy lips. He drove the length of his cock deep into her married pussy and began to lustily make love to her.

My wife put her hand on his muscular chest. "Whoa... Slow down, baby. Not so fast!" she told him. "My husband won't be done playing golf for hours. We don't need to be in any hurry!"

Nisha raised her head off the bed to kiss her young lover, her tongue sliding between his lips. She settled back onto the bed and shifted to a more comfortable position.

"This time... I want to tell *you* exactly how I want to be taken!"

Ankit smiled down at my wife and began to roll his hips against her, an amused smile on his lips. My wife and Ankit made love softly and slowly for the next hour or so, her young lover pulling long, strong orgasms out of her lithe body, Nisha panting and screaming profanities, writhing beneath his bulk, gleaming with sweat.

After he came in her for the third time, Nisha asked if she could use his shower. "So I don't smell like I've been making love!" she grinned.

Ankit had cameras in his bathroom and I watched as he took my wife from behind as she braced herself against the tiled walls, her heavy breasts swinging lewdly beneath her.

I felt empty as I turned off the computer, slumping down in my leather chair. I barely recognized the woman who had made love to Ankit with such abandon as my wife for the last so many years. I went out to my car and sat motionless in the seat.

My law firm was big. The financial consequences of a divorce would be devastating, not to mention the emotional impact it would have on me.

With my options limited, I resolved to somehow move past this, and focus on the future. I was probably playing way too much golf and my billable hours had gotten crazy. I could work on improving both these areas. Plus, I had detected nothing in Nisha's demeanour that would cause me to think this was nothing more than a one-time fling, something she had to get out of her system. Things were great at home, and in bed, and although I realized now where she had picked up her impressive oral skills, how could I complain about getting great head from my gorgeous, sexy wife? The decision made, I drove home.

Four weeks later

"Who are you going to dinner with?" I asked Nisha as she slipped into her sexy ankle strap sandals with the four-inch heels. She looked incredible in a navy, scooped neck dress that fit her slim body like a second skin, her cleavage proudly on display. Nisha walked to the mirror and started to apply a thick layer of shiny gloss to her pouty lips.

"Just Riya and some of the girls," she responded, studying herself closely in the mirror.

Riya lived a few streets over and was my wife's most attractive friend. I'd caught myself lusting after her at numerous parties. But she had a spotless reputation, a mom-of-the-year type, and was married to Nikhil, another friend of ours. I was glad my wife seemed to be spending more and more time with her.

I walked up behind Nisha and slid my hands across her firm tummy. I nuzzled her neck and took an earlobe gently between my lips.

"You know... we could send the kids out for pizza and you could tell the girls you've got a headache."

"You're so bad!" my wife grinned at me "Can I take a raincheck? I've been dying to try this new tapas place."

I kissed her on the back of the neck "Can't blame a guy for trying. Hey... will you be needing your checkbook? I need to update our accounts."

"No... I'll use my plastic. My checkbook's in my purse," she told me as I walked downstairs.

I opened my wife's purse and found her checkbook when I noticed a long, rectangular bulge in a side zip pocket. Nisha was still upstairs, so I quickly unzipped the pocket and was surprised to discover a hard pack of cigarettes and an expensive looking lighter. The thought of my wife smoking took me quickly back to the farmhouse and I got an awful feeling in the pit of my stomach. I heard my wife coming downstairs and I quickly returned the items to her purse.

Her high heels clicked on the hard wooden floor as she walked across the kitchen, throwing a small cosmetic bag in her purse.

"Bye sweetie!" she called brightly as she went out the door.

I walked to the front room and watched as her black Mercedes came down the driveway. She had her top down and our windows were open on a gorgeous late summer day. Nisha was already on her cell phone and I heard a throaty laugh and then she said, "I can't wait either, baby! I'll be there soon!" as she accelerated rapidly down the cul-de-sac.

One week later

When my secretary brought me the folder, I wasn't the least bit surprised. I ran a letter opener across the top and dumped its contents on my desk. Several mini-discs clattered on my desktop followed by a single, small piece of paper. The handwritten note said simply "You owe me twenty lakhs now".

The discs were dated from my wife's recent dinner with the girls. No set up this time, the video began with the image of my wife on her hands and knees, still wearing the dress and high heels I had watched her put on. I recognized Ankit, who had flipped her dress up over her tight little ass and was thrusting his thick shaft deep into her pussy as he kneeled behind her on a big leather couch.

I also recognized Riya as she sat off to one side, her legs crossed seductively, a short skirt riding high up a slender thigh. A glass of wine in one hand, a long, white cigarette between outstretched fingers in the other, she had a lewd smile on her face and you could hear her urging Ankit on.

Looks like Ankit has been a busy boy, my wife is a naughty girl and I am a poor man.

BIRTHDAY
TREAT

A rush was bored at work. With no new audit project in sight, he did not have a lot on his plate. To distract himself, he casually scrolled through the upcoming birthdays.

He was happy to see it was Diya's birthday week and her birthday was on Saturday. Diya was a co-worker and they had worked closely on many audit projects. Both of them were Chartered Accountants and had worked at the high-power audit firm for almost the same number of years. Arush was tall and good looking, but in a geeky sort of a way. He was, however, a confident charmer and totally knew how to turn a client's no to a yes. Diya was his exact opposite – introvert and shy, but dexterous in her work. She was beautiful with long auburn hair, but always hid her beautiful eyes behind her thick glasses.

Arush casually pinged Diya on the office messenger, asking if she was excited about the weekend, since it was her birthday.

Diya's response was pretty exciting. She was looking forward to her birthday – her 30th – which was a big one, but she had no plans as yet. She did not have many friends outside of work and since she stayed alone, she confessed she'd most likely end up all lonely on her birthday.

Arush immediately pounced on the opportunity and asked her if he could plan a surprise treat for her. She readily accepted. She asked him what the plan was, so she could work at it accordingly.

Arush had a nice lunch and more in mind. So he asked her to keep her afternoon and evening free for the treat. She was fine with it and wanted to know more about the plan. However, Arush kept it vague and told her that he will pick her up at around 12.30 from her house. The rest was a mystery and a surprise. She sounded sceptical, but he assured her that there was nothing to worry about.

Arush spent the next few days planning a romantic birthday treat for Diya in great detail. He had been hiding a crush on her for a long time and knew if he didn't take the lead, Diya would never get to know his feelings.

On Saturday, Arush reached Diya's home sharp at 12:30 to pick her up. He was wearing a sharp white shirt and jeans, while she was dressed up in a blue dress. Arush got down from the car and gave her a slight hug and wished her 'Happy Birthday'. He opened the door of the car for her, being a thorough gentleman.

Inside the car, Arush passed on a nice bouquet of roses that he had already got for her and wished her again. 'Diya, here's wishing you a very happy birthday. You landed on the earth from heaven on this day; you are as beautiful as an angel.'

Diya was flattered with the special treatment and the high praises. Her perfume was intoxicating to Arush as well. She asked him about the plan again. But instead, Arush said, "Sit back and enjoy! Today is about you and you must enjoy the day and leave the worries to me." Hearing this, Diya played along with a smile and sat back. She had never been treated so specially like this before.

They drove to a nice restaurant on the outskirts of the city. They were chit-chatting about various topics all through the way. Suddenly it started drizzling and the weather became very romantic. Arush slowly slid his hand across the gear box and held Diya's hand, saying, 'The heaven is weeping as they are missing their most beautiful angel.' Just as he gave her hand a squeeze, Diya went red in the face and blushed. Her pink cheeks made her look even more desirable to Arush.

Soon, they reached the restaurant and were received by the maître d', who already knew the whole plan. They were taken to a special table at the back of the restaurant, set in a garden. The whole path was decorated with beautiful flowers and lily petals were sprinkled on the path already. As they reached the table, they saw two waiters holding a big sign saying HAPPY BIRTHDAY DIYA and another waiter holding a cake.

Diya was over the moon and clutched Arush's hand tightly in hers. She was giddy with happiness and was falling all over him. They soon sat at the table and cut the cake. She gave him a quick peck on his cheek as she fed him a piece of cake, saying, "This is the best birthday cake ever." He saw a look of love and emotion in her eyes and knew he was going in the right direction.

They popped open a bottle of red wine, which was specially kept for them. They ordered some food while they sipped their wine and were lost in each other. They forgot the whole world and were just lost in each other's eyes and words. Arush reached out and held her hand across the table and said, "I am glad you let me be a part of your special day."

Diya blushed and said, "You are the one who made it a special day."

With the sun setting in the background, Arush wondered out aloud, "How can you be so beautiful? The beauty around us pales in comparison." Diya just blushed and her pink cheeks beckoned Arush. He reached out and brushed a strand hair off her cheek and kissed her lightly on the cheek.

Diya looked up and was flustered. Arush pressed his advantage and asked, "How was the treat? I hope I was able to make the day special and memorable for you."

She said, "I am flattered with the special treatment. This was definitely one of the best birthday treats I have ever had." She was clearly happy about the time spent with him.

On seeing her so happy, Arush asked her, "What is my return gift, birthday girl?"

She thought for a second and said, "Make a wish and it shall be fulfilled."

Arush looked deep into her eyes and asked her, "Since the day I saw you, I always wanted to taste your red rosy lips with mine. That would be the best return gift for me."

Diya was shocked for a second and then hit Arush in the arm and said, "Stop being naughty and ask for a proper gift."

Arush said, "I am not teasing you. I have wanted this gift for a long time now. It would be the best return gift I can have from you."

Diya looked embarrassed, but Arush could sense she was not totally against the idea. Arush gently reached out and touched her hand with his. He said, "It is ok if you don't want to. But you should know that this has indeed been my greatest wish for a long time."

Diya hesitated and then agreed to his demand with a demure nod of her head. However, she said, "I will give you your return gift, but I don't feel comfortable enough here. Can we go someplace a bit more private?"

Arush did not hesitate a bit longer, and immediately asked for the bill. Clearing the dues with a flourish of his credit card, they headed out. He asked Diya, "I have parked the car in a secluded area of the parking lot. I think I can have the return gift there?"

Diya just nodded her head lightly and Arush was on cloud nine. He escorted her to their car, where there was no one around to watch them. He held the door open as she entered his car and he went and sat next to her in the driver's seat. He was looking at her intently as they sat in the car for a few minutes.

She suddenly pulled Arush by his hand and quickly gave him a small 2-second smooch and left him back in his seat.

Arush was clearly disappointed. He said it in as many words too. "That was way too quick and was done before I could even react or relish it." He retaliated, "This is not done. It's a return gift and you need to let me enjoy the same to my content and not make it so short and quick."

She sat back in her seat and thought for a second. Then she leaned in a bit and said, "Then come on and enjoy the return gift as you wish." This was what Arush wanted to hear. He leaned into her and slid his hand behind her head into her hair. He started with slowly pressing his lips onto hers.

Arush started kissing her slowly in a romantic way, his hand in her hair while the other gripped her waist. She hesitated at first, but then responded with passion and their tongues started to tango with each other. Arush's hands were roaming in her hair. The heat was turning up with each second that passed.

After what felt like an eternity but was actually just 3-4 minutes, she broke the kiss and sat back in her seat with a naughty smile on her face. Arush was about to start the car when she grabbed him by his head and started to kiss him again, wildly. It was like a wild cat that had tasted blood and unleashed herself.

He was stunned for a second, but then started to enjoy the wet surprise from her. Now Arush's hand was roaming around freely on her back. He pulled her up by her ass and was enjoying kissing her to the core. Another few minutes of passionate kissing and she pulled back, sitting in her seat.

He was stunned at the turn of events. Without another moment, he revved up the car and started driving towards the city. He was stealing glances of her rosy lips or her bosom in between the drive, and she noticed that. Soon after, she slowly crawled her hand towards his hand and rubbed her hand on his.

She looked into his eyes and asked, "Was it too much for you to handle or can you handle some more heat?"

In response, Arush asked her, "Where can I show you how much I can handle?"

She directed Arush towards her apartment. They reached the location, quietly got down from the car and entered the flat without catching much attention. Diya went inside first, and Arush followed inside locking the door. As soon as he turned, Diya jumped on him, wrapped her legs around his waist and started kissing him like a wild cat.

Arush was holding her by her ass for support and squeezing it at times and feeling her round buns. They both were playing wildly with their tongues and kissing each other like there was no tomorrow. He took her to the bedroom, holding her in the air, and threw her on the bed. She quickly got up and pulled him on the bed.

She said, "Lie down and enjoy the return gift." She slowly started to tease him and strip herself. The slow movement from her hips was making her look even sexier. She slid out of her dress in a sensuous swift move and looked like a red-hot devil in her red lingerie. She removed that too, swinging her sultry body to some unheard music playing in my head.

She gave Arush the exclusive look that many people in the office had been dreaming of. She came down onto him and pushed his shirt upwards. She then started licking and kissing around his navel sensuously. Slowly, she was opening all the buttons of the shirt one by one. She was kissing every inch of his body from the navel till his nipples.

She came up and gave a nice hard love bite on his right nipple and hissed, "Inspecting and marking my territory." She started sucking his nipples, biting them in between and smashing the other nipple between her fingers. It was a different type of pleasure he had never felt before. Her fingernails were scratching all over his torso, leaving marks while she was sucking and biting on his nipples. She kept on slobbering his chest while her nails roamed free on his chest leaving marks on his body.

She crawled upwards, licking him from the nipple through the shoulder to the neck till the ear. She whispered, "Are you enjoying the return gift Arush?"

Arush could just nod in affirmation. She removed his shirt completely and started kissing him all over. This was beyond his wildest expectations, where he had thought she would be demure and docile in bed. Her lips made their way down to his navel and were kissing him there.

Arush started caressing her ass and started spanking her ass nice and hard to make her white ass red. She started moaning for each spank she got on her ass and that drove Arush wilder. Diya was enjoying the feel of his rough hands on her ass, as they spanked her and made her red. She moaned in pleasure. "Ohhhh Arusshhhhhhhhh, that's it. Hit me harder." Hearing this, Arush spanked her even more while she enjoyed in pleasure. Her lips and teeth doing a number on his torso, while her fingers digging into his flesh.

He suddenly pushed her down onto the bed and went down kissing her on her red crimson lips. She kissed him back with ferocity and bit his lips. He could feel a world of pleasure as she sucked on his lips hungrily. He disengaged from her lips and moved to her neck as he bit her slowly and lightly. She moaned his name in pleasure, all the while her hands on his back. He moved down to her cleavage and reached her big boobs. He slowly kissed them both one by one and then bit her nipples. He could feel her nipples go hard under his tongue and kept licking and biting them.

He pulled her up into his lap on the corner of the bed and started sucking her firm boobs while facing him. He was sucking one of her boobs nice and hard, giving love bites at times while pinching and smashing the other nipple with fingers. He knew she was turned on and wanted to feel her now. He turned her around so that he was facing her from behind, and kissed her sensuous back. He slowly made her bend forward and spread her legs apart. He could see her flower clearly in front of him, wet and dripping with her love juices.

He slowly caressed the opening causing her to moan out loud. He kissed her ass and then slowly pushed in his middle finger inside her already wet pussy. As he slid in smoothly, she gave out a low long moan of pleasure. He knew she needed it. So he slowly started fingering her nice and deep while kissing her all over the neck and shoulders from behind. He started to rub his thumb on the opening of her pussy in a circular manner. He was slowly stimulating her. His fingers were wet with her juices in no time. Arush started massaging her puffed-up pussy which made her buck against him. She kept moaning out loud, clearly enjoying every bit, and wanting more from him.

Arush asked her, "Do you want more?" and kissed her neck again. She moaned her approval as he bit her while his finger stimulated her. He slowly pushed in a second finger and started stroking her in a to and fro motion. His fingers were touching her core while his thumb was stimulating her clit. He continued for a few minutes and hit her core. He knew that this would take her to her peak and continued with it. Within a couple of minutes, she was cumming in pleasure and moaned out loud. Arush had to taste her, so he put his head between her fleshy thighs. He removed his fingers and thrust his face between her legs. He loved the musky aroma of her pussy and started eating her, his face getting sticky with her juices. He was slurping her as she was discharging and his tongue was skilfully entering her. She rocked up and down on the bed with pleasure as she felt his soft tongue stimulate hitherto untouched corners of her pussy. This was too much for her and soon she came all over again, this time on his face.

She turned around and started rubbing his already hard cock over his underwear and pressing his balls nice and hard. Slowly she removed the underwear and gently brushed her fingertips up the shaft of his penis and enjoyed watching it bounce excitedly. His back was already arching at this point and eyes rolling in pleasure. A tingle stirred her clit. She curled her fingers around his rock hard erection and gently moved up and down, letting his penis travel in her loose grip. Continuing the steady pace, working his shaft with her fingers curled around, she lowered her mouth to that shiny tip. Her tongue darted out to taste that shiny surface with a salty tang and she savoured that first connection with her mouth. Her tongue swirled over it as her hand continued its movements, and her other hand found his balls and started to tease and pull gently on them to add to the sensations he was feeling. Enjoying this early tease, Diya let the tight circle of her lips meet the tip of his penis and slowly roll them downwards, letting her mouth water more at the thoughts and sensations happening in her mind and body so as to lubricate her lips' journey down his shaft.

Bringing the circle of her lips back up to his cock tip and having her hand resume its attentions on his shaft, she finally got her tongue into action. She began the slight suction letting the insides of her cheeks touch his penis shaft as she travelled downwards while sucking him off. Her left hand was toying with his balls, massaging and gently pulling downwards, which caused him to stiffen to the maximum in her mouth. In between, she would press his balls hard and enjoy the loud moaning. As Diya sucked and glided, she heard him panting and calling her name. She was more turned on with that.

She took his full length so his cock-head hit the back of her throat with every thrust. Arush held her hair as her head moved back and forth on him. She was gagging and choking on his dick, but she was enjoying this feeling. She kept stroking him with her hand while her tongue licked him furiously. His breath was becoming shallower. She wasn't finished with that penis yet. Her cunt was desperate to feel it inside her.

Arush was thrusting and bucking madly inside Diya's mouth and just when he came to the point of release, Diya pulled her mouth away and, spreading her pussy lips, straddled him. She started riding atop him, jumping on his cock, thrusting her nipples into his mouth. He tasted each of her nipples until they were glistening with his saliva. Arush's free hand slid along her ass crack, and he fondled Diya's cheeks, pushing a finger into her rear centre of pleasure, feeling her muscles contracting and releasing alternately. "Oh Arush!!" She cried out, arching her back. "Aahh…" She moaned again gripping his shoulder. His thrust was meeting hers, making him go deeper inside her.

She finally started squeezing his cock with her muscles down there and he came, shuddering, endlessly inside her, his body trembling with the force of the release. Arush bit down hard on her nipples as she relished her third orgasm, leaking her juices all over his cock. "You feel so good," she whispered.

They both lay down for a bit, holding each other. Then Diya turned towards him and went on all four, in the ubiquitous doggy style and looked at him and said in an alluring voice, "Make this wild cat moan louder now."

Arush went down on her and started licking her crack, from her pussy till her asshole and made her wet with his tongue. His tongue was penetrating her and touching her walls. He started licking her asshole wet and inserted two fingers into her pussy, ramming it deep and hard. This time he was not being gentle. He kept on going hard and fast as she moaned his name in pleasure. After a while, when he knew she was really wet, he lay down and brought her pussy onto his face.

He started eating her pussy and pushed his tongue deep inside her. He knew she liked it by the way her legs contracted around his face. He tried inserting his middle finger into her anal hole and pushed it in slowly. She moaned like anything with pleasure as he was stimulating her on both ends at the same time. He kept eating her for a couple of minutes, while his fingers penetrated her anal sphincter. He kept doing until she came again suddenly on his face and he drank all her juices till the last drop.

He positioned her back on all fours again, and slowly inserted his organ deep into her wet pussy in one go. She moaned with pleasure as he slid inside her and he started ramming her pussy nice and deep. He went into her deep and hard and thrust into her hard. She gasped and shut her eyes. It felt as if something inside her was slowly working its way through the organ into her. He was going deep into her pussy to the maximum and she was enjoying the pleasure. He started to go a little harder and faster when her moans came more often. Arush had never felt so much pleasure before. He leaned over and held her by her hair and her shoulder and rammed into her hard. He wanted to reach her core and make her feel the ultimate pleasure of the world. He was plunging inside her, hitting her in the spot that turned her moans into one long, high-pitched orgasm.

After a couple of minutes of thrusting into her pussy nice and hard, he knew he was about to come, but he wanted to prolong the pleasure for him and her. He pulled out of her and spanked her ass. Diya was surprised and jerked up in pleasure. He took advantage and slapped her ass harder and they became red. Diya moaned with pleasure as she felt his rough hands on her ass, pleasuring her. She looked back over her shoulder and said in a sexy manner, "Please finish it now Arush. Don't prolong it anymore. I want it inside now."

Arush knew he needed to finish her off and pushed his cock deeper inside Diya. Her sheath opened up and accepted him inside him. He thrust in deep and penetrated her. Her body began to jerk and shudder in response to his thrust. Arush knew he was about to come soon and pushed in harder and deeper. Diya let out her high keening call and Arush felt an abrupt rush of his seminal-fluid, racing through him like a river, not slowing down. He grabbed hold of her boobs and he arched himself toward her as he came. He could feel Diya also coming along with him and her juices mixed with his.

They didn't move for a few moments, needing to catch their breath. She snuggled up inside his arms with her boobs pressing against his chest. Diya was nibbling his nipple while they just cuddled against each other.

Arush smiled and asked her, "How was the birthday treat?"

She smiled, came up, kissed him and said, "The return gift was much more pleasurable."

FALLING
IN
LOVE

Keshav saw Suparna for the first time at Pune airport. It was a usual July evening. He was waiting at the baggage counter with his family when he heard a divine sound - lovely pearls of laughter, which strung a chord in his heart.

He turned around to take a quick glance. She spotted her instantly and her light brown intense and expressive eyes took away his heart at the the first sight. Suparna had dark brown hair, neatly tied up in a ponytail which ended up in perfect curls. She had the perfect feminine features comprised of light brown eyes, a small nose, light pink lips and everything else of the right size in the right places. She oozed of confidence and poise. She was enough to mesmerize him.

He glanced at her.

He found her looking at him too.

He smiled.

She smiled back.

For the first time in his life, Keshav felt weak at his knees. He realized what having butterflies in stomach actually meant. He never believed in love at first sight. But now, he did.

His heart was beating faster and he was trying to figure out a way to approach her. But before he could gather the courage to do so, she went away with her family. He was still stuck waiting for his luggage.

Keshav skipped his heartbeat again when he saw her at the reception of the same hotel where he was staying. While he was checking into the hotel with his family, he heard the familiar sound again. He turned around and saw her walking with her parents into one of the lifts. While he wanted to rush and check the floor number they got off at, his Father called him for help. Once again he couldn't talk to her.

Keshav had come to Pune to join a prestigious engineering college. He had worked diligently to clear the tough entrance exam and was looking forward to the next four years of learning and fun. However, his heart and mind were elsewhere now. He wasn't able to resist thinking about that girl. In fact, it was her charisma that was pulling him towards her. Like that girl, Keshav was also with her family. But he wished he would have been on a trip with his friends, at least they would have helped or at least given ideas to approach her.

Keshav was lost in his beautiful thoughts when his dad called him, "Get ready or we will be late for your college."

The thought of living away from his family and the new found freedom was giving butterflies in his stomach. But his eyes were still searching for one look of that angel he had seen twice since last night. But she was nowhere to be seen now.

'Must have gone for sightseeing with her family.' He wondered.

It was like a festival at the college. Students from across the country had gathered to join a new chapter of their life.

Keshav's happiness knew no bounds when he saw his angel again. He couldn't believe his eyes. He rubbed and blinked his eyes to make sure it was her standing in the queue. A smile crept on his face and his eyes shone as the electric wave ran across his nerves.

'Thank you God. Now I only wish she joins electronic engineering and be my classmate.'

But once more he missed her as she vanished while he had his eyes closed praying to god.

'Fuck man! I could have prayed without closing my eyes. Now where would I find her? And how would I know if she is taking admission here or came to accompany her brother who was there at the airport and hotel with her.' Keshav cursed himself.

The first day of joining formalities was over. Keshav's college was not far from the hotel where he was staying with his family. He was excited for his new college life and a little curious about her. He excused himself from his parent's company to explore the campus and search for his angel. However, it was to no avail.

Tired, Keshav walked back to the hotel room and collapsed on the bed. His phone rang to wake him up.

"Where are you Keshav? You are not even opening your door. We are waiting for you at the restaurant for dinner," his dad called.

"Oops. Sorry dad. I will be there in the next five minutes." he replied and hung up.

Keshav washed his face, got ready and rushed to join his parents for the supper.

"Here is my son, Keshav. He joined electronic engineering. Keshav, meet Suparna. She has joined your college only. Computer Science. They are also from Uttarakhand."

Keshav was mesmerized listening to his dad's words.

"Really? Great! Nice meeting you," Keshav replied, trying to be a decent guy.

"Keshav, she is going to stay away from her family for the first time. She is so innocent. Please take care of Suparna," her father said.

'I don't know if she is innocent but she is definitely sweet. Sweet like any dessert.' Keshav thought to himself, but all he could say was, "Sure uncle. Always!"

Keshav was on cloud nine thanking the elders for initiating his love story.

* * *

Next morning Keshav and Suparna moved in to their allotted hostel rooms. Suparna was waving goodbye to her mom, dad and brother with drops of tears ready to roll down her cheeks. Keshav was looking at her from a distance. He had already said goodbye to his parents and they were on their way back. He walked over to her.

"Hey, are you practicing for your vidai?" he asked touching her shoulder. A rush of warmth spread through her veins at his touch.

"What?" She reacted.

"Why do you girls cry so much? See the positive things which will make you extremely happy." He suggested.

"Like what?"

"Like what you will wear for the first class tomorrow morning. How many new friends you can make! Maybe you can think about the possibility of meeting your prince charming."

She giggled. "So what are you excited about?" she asked.

"Well, I am excited about everything. It is a new life to experience and to create memories forever with my new friends."

"Seems like you already got your friends here."

"Till now only one, standing in front of me."

She laughed, a sound which set off the chords of his heart. She looked, prettier while laughing showing off a set of cute dimples.

He looked at her and their gazes locked. Despite the cool weather, the temperature in the atmosphere had shot up a few degrees. A warm rush flooded over him, and he felt his heart race in his chest. Keshav felt an instant rise in his testosterone. He instantly knew she was the one.

The next few weeks were spent settling into their new hostel schedule, making new friends and attending classes. Keshav however left no chance unturned to be around Suparna and soon their budding friendship solidified. Suparna and Keshav started spending more time together than with their other friends. Keshav would feel butterflies fluttering in his tummy and his heart pounding whenever he saw her. When he was not with her he would be dreaming about her.

The college fest was fast approaching and Suparna decided to take part in the dance competition. The rules specified that each dance was to be a couple dance and the partner couldn't be of the same gender. Suparna asked Keshav to be her partner. Keshav agreed, after all he could not break her heart.

They would spend all their free time practicing a fast contemporary number which was Suparna's choice. The fast moves, the physical closeness and heavy breathing brought many deep feelings in Keshav's heart. He decided to proclaim his love to Suparna on the night of the fest.

Soon the evening of the fest was there and they were called onto the stage. There chemistry was all for to watch and their dance sizzled. After the dance Keshav pulled Suparna to a side backstage and said, "Suparna, ever since the day I first saw you at the airport, I have been in love with you. Will you be my girlfriend?"

Suparna looked at him in shock. An announcement on the stage followed by loud cheers from the crowd hid her answer from Keshav. Suddenly they were surrounded by a bunch of their friends congratulating them for winning the dance competition. As they were pulled on to the stage to accept their prize, Keshav saw tears in Suparna's eyes but heard that beautiful sound of her laugh. She looked back at him and repeated, "YES".

Soon Keshav and Suparna were the hottest couple in college. They could be seen holding hands between classes or hugging and kissing each other in dark corners of the campus. While Keshav wanted to explore more, Suparna did not allow him to do anything more than play with her body a bit. Keshav's raging testosterone wanted him to go ahead but Suparna was a bit shy and she wanted their first time to be special. Keshav had to be happy with touching her over her clothes and tasting the sweet nectar of her lips.

Soon a friend of Keshav announced that he was throwing his 19th birthday party at a farmhouse near Mulshi Dam. The farmhouse, even though owned by his parents, would be empty of adult supervision and booze would be flowing. Keshav was invited with Suparna for the party.

They all left early on a Saturday morning on their bikes and reached by lunch time. The weather was beautiful and so was the company.

The music of water flowing could be easily heard from the farm house. They all had a hearty lunch along with some beer and whisky. While Keshav could hold his drink Suparna was a light drinker. She felt a little dizzy and wanted to clear her head.

"Shall we go out and see around?" Suparna asked Keshav. The view and earthy fragrance of the place reminded her of the beauty of her hometown.

"Of course. Let's finish lunch and then we can go for a walk." He assured her.

Everyone was tired and was feeling so sleepy after a long drive, lunch and drinks. Except Suparna and Keshav, rest all decided to take an afternoon nap to charge up for the night party.

However, Keshav was happy that no one is there to disturb them. Suparna was also happy to get some alone time with her love.

Holding hands together, they walked a little far away from the farm house. Suparna was looking alluring in her olive-green silk cropped top and blue lacy skirt that barely covered her knees. Keshav was comfortable in his black t-shirt and beige shorts.

Keshav held Suparna closely. "Isn't the scenery as beautiful as you?" He said looking into her eyes.

Suparna blushed. Her pink lips pulled upward into a wide smile.

"Would you like to sit here for some time?" He asked pointing towards a place under a big tree. There was also a big rock nearby giving them little privacy. Apart from the sound of flowing water, cool breeze and occasional chirping of birds, there was no other sound. The place was so calm and the view was breathtaking.

"I love spending time with you. Looking into your eyes, in your arms. Everything feels so good and warm." Suparna said snuggling into him.

"I too love being with you all the time." Keshav said moving closer to her and tucked a curl behind her ear. The feel of Keshav's touch made her shiver. Keshav's heart was racing. She could hear every breath he took. She moved her face close to his. Her cheeks turned red hot. His arms wrapped around her waist and pulled her closer to his chest. They both could feel warm and deep breathing of each other and their desires were steaming. He cupped her face and brushed his nose against hers. He could feel the trembling sound of her pounding heart. He slightly angled his head to the side. His lips came closer and closer to hers. His breath was rhyming with that of hers. Suparna closed her eyes.

Her body tingled with excitement as Keshav's lips tenderly covered hers. She felt his tender love with the touch of his lips. She responded parting her mouth and let his tongue explore hers. She tasted like honey and Keshav loved it. Their lips and tongues met with a fierceness driven by the intensity of the moment. They both were kissing passionately. Their tongues were swirling, curling and dancing together. His wet lips trailed from her mouth down to the neckline of her top. There were trails of sparks with every kiss and touch. She quivered under his touch.

Few minutes later, Keshav broke the sizzling kiss and gazed into her eyes longingly. Her heart thundered and he caressed her bare waist through his hands under her silky crop top. Neither he said anything nor she stopped him. She pulled him closer, hugging him tightly. Their bodies pressing each other. He kissed her harder on her neck, shoulder and upper part of her bare bosom. He kissed her down to her soul. There was love and excitement.

He moved his hand over her satin smooth thighs, caressing them slowly. His one hand was searching for something under her short skirt. He pulled the string of her satin panty. Her heartbeat increased as she experienced the warm sensation all over her body. She hesitated and held his hand stopping to explore further. Keshav looked into her eyes, longingly and said, "I will stop if you want me to. This has to be your choice. But today I don't want to stop darling." He nuzzled the side of her neck. His hot breath and kisses and the sound of his voice sent a shiver through her body. She looked into his eyes, filled with love for her and she surrendered her body and soul to him.

He moved his lips to the side of her neck and started kissing and nibbling. Suparna bit her lip with satisfaction. His thumb was encircling her clit, teasing her tender womanhood. Keshav slid his middle finger inside of her. Her tensed hips lifted off the ground. He groaned feeling how aroused she was. He pushed his finger inside her hot pool, parting the hymen. She squirmed against him. He answered each of her moans, teasing her, slowly stroking her, reaching deeper and deeper with his fingertips while occasionally darting in and out. His hand found her wet hole begging to be invaded. His middle finger was probing, backing off looking for that elusive g-spot. Suddenly he hit it and Suparna cried out. "Oh god, oh, oh my god." Her desire flooded to the surface. The orgasm hit her like a tidal wave. She moaned in ecstasy.

Keshav stopped for a moment and grazed into her eyes. He saw the love she felt for him and saw his own love reflected in it. She leaned forward and kissed him on his lips deep. He murmured, "I love you Suparna."

She replied, "I love you even more." They broke the spell and he started teasing her g-spot again. She was wet and leaking her juice's on his hands.

Exhausted, Suparna hugged Keshav, breathing heavily.

"Keshav," she whispered.

"What?" he asked in a soft tone of voice. His eyes met hers.

"Keshav," she breathed against her lips. "I want you now."

Keshav's heart exploded. He felt hot and hard. He was itching to feel her, to make love to her. He pulled her towards him while his back resting on the tree. She sat on his lap with her legs parted straddling him on top. They were sitting upright, facing each other, with Suparna on top of his lap with her legs on his sides.

She pulled off his t-shirt. He slipped his hand on her back under her top unhooking the bra. He ran his hand all over her back down to her waist, moving towards her stomach. His every stroke and kiss was like a blissful eternity for her. The last of her self- control melted away when he touched her soft bosoms. It was the first experience of being touched by a boy on her bare body. She had never felt like this before. She closed her eyes, feeling every moment.

Keshav lifted her green silk top and was awestruck seeing her creamy soft and naked jiggling breasts. They were like beautiful aroused peaks, throbbing with need. He cupped a breast in each hand, gently kneading and stroking her aching breasts, sending out little waves of pleasure throughout her entire body, like ripples flowing in the water.

She squealed and whimpered arching back. His hands ran down her stomach while he nuzzled the side of her throat. His wet lips and tongue were exploring every part of her skin. She was moaning with every kiss and every touch.

Keshav buried his face between her bobbing breasts and pressed the sides tightly against his cheeks while moving his head back and forth. Her purple swollen nipples were erect with desire. Keshav captured it with his tongue. He pinched the hard little tips between his teeth. He sucked it gently while she groaned softly, eyes closed and lips slightly apart. She wrapped her arms around his neck. At that moment it didn't matter that they were in a public place and might get caught, she wanted him more than anything.

"You are so beautiful." He whispered in her ear.

She felt it. More beautiful than she had ever felt in her life. Waves of pleasure were surging through her.

As he sucked her nipples, he held her hands guiding her to his engorged manhood. Using both her hands she unbuttoned and unzipped his shorts, pulled his underwear away. She was amazed to see the hard magnificent arousal for the first time. She stroked and massaged his erect masculinity. She knew he was ready to penetrate into her dripping wet pussy. He slid her skirt up over her hips, removing her underwear. Keshav lifted her with his hands and pulled her on top his tool. As she lowered herself on him, he buried his hard arousal slowly, inch by inch, inside the warmth between her legs. Suparna was moaning, obeying an instinct she hadn't known she possessed. She wrapped her legs around his waist, widening her hips to meet the possessive thrusting, willing to take him further and deeper inside of her. Keshav gripped her waist with his hands controlling the movements. It was overwhelming for both of them, but neither Keshav nor Suparna wanted it to stop. Keshav groaned and sped up his thrusting, leaned forward and started sucking her breasts. Full of desire, she writhed in pleasure, clenching to him as he filled her. She gasped, closing her eyes as his complete manhood was inside her.

Keshav was pumping faster, sending shocks of pleasure through her body. He closed his eyes, throwing his head back, letting out a long moan as he drove into her as hard as he could. He knew he was almost done. While this was his first time, he couldn't hold back anymore after looking at his beautiful goddess. Orgasm shuddered through him. They lied down on the grass next to each other.

"Your eyes telling me that you enjoyed it," Keshav whispered.

"Very much!" Her eyes shone. The grin on her face was indicating something was still going on in her mind.

Suparna ran her hands up to his face, kissed his lips. She began kissing slowly on the right side of his neck, nibbling and sucking the soft skin, leaving the purple bite marks. She murmured, "You might be done, my love, but I am not done yet. I need more of you again. Soon." She kissed his neck again, biting lightly, leaving small marks all the way to his shoulder. She reached for his now flaccid tool and started playing with it. Jerking it between her hands. Keshav lay on his back looking up in the sky enjoying the best day of his life. Suparna jolted him out of his reverie by suddenly biting his nipples. He groaned in pleasure as he felt her body press against him playing with him. She was jerking his manhood slowly between her soft hands, slowly and steadily making it come to life. She bent down suddenly and kissed the tip of his cock and licked it lightly. She moved back up and looked into his eye. He saw her naked desire and hot blood flushed through him. She felt him hardening again against her belly. Keshav groaned and held her tightly, biting on her neck, this time leaving his mark on her.

He pulled her towards him and made her lay next to him. He rolled up and over her, holding himself up on his arms as he slipped between her legs and positioned himself at the wetness at her center. Suparna quivered as he brushed against her and pressed into entrance of her femininity. She wanted him to enter her deep, so she lifted and wrapped her legs around his neck. Leaning forward he slid into her, and she gasped at this new sensation. Keshav groaned as the hot warmth of her cunt clasped at his cock. He thrust inside her, slowly at first and then a little faster as she began to relax. Suparna bit her lower lip. "Deeper," she moaned and lifted higher. Pleasure was burning along her nerves. His hands massaging and squeezing her boobs, fondling and pulling her tits. He held her snugly, constantly thrusting.

The muscles of her slick wetness constricted around his dick as she shook in oblivion. He was thrusting his hardness into her softness, filling her deep inside. She arched off the floor as the sweet lava of their love flowed inside her with the wild wave of ultimate pleasure. He held her face by her hair and kissed her hard while constantly thrusting into her. Suparna let out a low moan at the pleasure engulfing her. She was still clutching him closer and scratched his back with her nails. He grew wilder at this act and started moving with renewed vigor as they shivered against each other. She was clinging to him, releasing the hot fluid of her maidenhood in pleasure. She came and her discharge was all over his hard cock which continued to thrust inside her. She shivered in pleasure as she explored the pleasures of maidenhood.

Keshav was still not done and kept thrusting in her as her orgasm subsided. His deep thrust drew a light scream, equal part pleasure and pain from her. Keshav stopped a little worried and asked, "Honey did I hurt you?" She replied, "No you didn't but I think I just finished. Also I am afraid that I am not in my safe period and we don't have any protection with us" Keshav understood her point and immediately withdrew from her. He did not want this moment of love to become something they would come to regret later. He stood up, his throbbing hard cock a sign of his unsatisfied needs, and said, "I understand sweetheart. Let's stop for now. I will be more careful for future."

She sat up and pulled him back. "Keshav, wait." She sat on her thighs and held his rod in one hand, stroking his throbbing cock while playing with her sweetly curved boobs with another hand. Keshav was extremely excited with the scene. She leaned in and opened her lips, using her tongue she tasted his hard loins. He felt her wet tongue on his pulsating manhood. His heart began beating erratically in anticipation of her hot tongue was working its magic. When she heard his moan, she opened her mouth wide and took him in. She moved her mouth tenderly back and forth over Keshav's cock. Then slowly sucked his cock into her mouth, as deep as she could take it, and then slowly out again. His moans became louder, "My god, Suparna, Oh god."

He bent over slightly, overwhelmed by the sensation of his cock sliding over her tongue to the back of her throat and then out again. He held her head by her hair and gently pushed her deeper after several more strokes. Keshav loved all the sensations he was experiencing. She took him as deep as she could and he felt the back of her throat touch his cock. Suparna determined to give him supreme pleasure and kept going until she was gagging on his long length of meat. She stopped and took him out and slapped it between her breasts. She held it tightly between her boobs and moved it up and down. Keshav felt heavenly between her soft boobs and beautiful touch. Seeing the look of pleasure on his face, she licked the top of his cock head and took it in her mouth again. The feeling of warmth after the soft touch was too much for Keshav. Soon his body was tensing as he exploded with pleasure and he bit his lip as his body jerked. Suparna took his seed inside her mouth, as he jerked and let loose. She felt beautiful as she knew she had satisfied her lover, just like he had satisfied her a few moments ago.

After finally climaxing he fell onto her, sweaty and panting. Keshav rolled down next to her. They were lying on the grass and Suparna rested her head on his arm. There was so much to say but they both were too exhausted to speak. After few minutes of just lying, Keshav lifted his head up resting on one elbow and looked into her sparkling eyes with a satisfied smile.

"It just happened! I am still to believe it really happened." Suparna giggled.

"It is so crazy. I agree. But this was so special." He kissed her forehead, her eyelids, her cheeks, her neck.

"What about the birthday party?" Keshav mumbled between the kisses.

"There is nothing wrong with following trend of reaching late."

A smile of bliss and satisfaction scattered on their face.

It was already getting dark. They slipped back into their clothes and walked towards the party venue, their hands grasped tightly together. Hickeys scattered across their necks, chests and boobs and grins on their faces.

INSTA-LOVE

"Ping! Ping!" The sound of notification on her phone distracted Riya from the fashion magazine she was reading. A fashionista by nature, she had walked the ramp in her college fest fashion shows and her all year round dressing sense was still the talking point of her college alumni group chat.

Riya opened the app and saw that she had received another 100 likes on the recent picture she had posted on Instagram and quite a few comments. However the notification sound was from a DM she had received. While she was used to ignoring most DM's this one was from someone special – her Insta friend and off late Insta-crush – Suhas.

Riya blushed when she read the message – "Your beauty is nothing compared to my love. Though I wish this pic was only for me to see and not the whole world."

She replied back cheekily - "Beauty should be for the world to see, not kept hidden." and logged out of the app. She knew it was time for Ritesh, her husband to be back from work and he did not like being disturbed by the incessant notifications. In fact, of late, it felt there was nothing he liked - her food, her chatter or her company.

Riya was like one of the many bored housewives in the big city Mumbai, alone at home, while her husband was at work all day. She had grown up in a smaller city and the rush of Mumbai was something she was yet to get used to. Growing up, she knew she had both beauty and brains. Her friends in school and college always told her that. While she got the attention of all the boys in her college, she never got involved with anyone. She knew how conservative her parents were and she did not want to hamper her chances at getting an advanced education.

However fate and her parents had other plans for her. They set her up for marriage as soon as her graduation ended.

The memory of the first time she met Ritesh was still fresh in her mind. He came wearing a white crisp shirt, blue denims and a pair of aviators stuck to his shirt pocket. He looked dashing and handsome, was courteous to her family and was soft spoken. When they were given the space to meet and talk privately, the first thing he asked her was - "So what do you want in a husband?"

She immediately blurted out, "An equal partner."

He laughed at her answer and joked, "Definitely what I want in my wife."

They both grinned and soon a steady flow of conversation ensued. Riya demurely nodded her head when her parents asked her opinion about the alliance.

They had a quick marriage and an even quicker honeymoon at the Maldives. The wedding ceremony was a blur and they left for their honeymoon via a short stopover in Mumbai. Ritesh had gotten the bare minimum of 10 days off for his marriage. He had been living in Mumbai for the past 5 years and was working in a bank at a senior position. While it entailed a lot of perks, it also meant he had no time for himself.

The time spent in Mauritius was like a dream in heaven. The resort and the scenery were beautiful, though the love birds hardly had time to soak in the beauty of nature. Riya lost her virginity amidst the beautiful sea in the honeymoon suite of their cottage. Ritesh was tender and relentless when he was in bed with her, driving into her like a drill in search for the oceans bottom. He woke her sexuality with his intense love making. He spent all three days, pleasuring her and teaching her what pleasure was. Just when Riya started enjoying and learning what her man liked in bed, it was time for them to go back home.

However coming back home was like being brought to the reality of life. As soon as they were back home, Ritesh fell back to his work grind, leaving Riya unquenched. Riya spent the first couple of months trying to adjust to her new life and also trying to spark some desire in her husband. But Ritesh was too tired to pay any attention to her. He also did not like her idea of studying more and said, "We just got married. Take a year off, there is nothing to lose. You can apply next year, when the new session starts. Also what is the hurry, you stay at home and relax."

It was 9 at night and the usual time for Ritesh to arrive. Riya had just finished garnishing the dinner. She greeted him and asked, "Darling how was your day?"

"It was fine, like usual." Ritesh grunted back as he went in to freshen up.

He was out in sometime, in his night clothes and sat at the dining table. He was used to be served by Riya, who demurely served him hot food and a fresh glass of whisky. He downed his first peg immediately and while she refilled, he started eating. He did not even wait for Riya to start eating and was done soon. While Riya was eating in silence, he sat in front of the TV nursing his 3rd drink of the night watching news aloud.

Soon Riya was done and joined him on the couch. She leaned on his shoulder and kissed his cheek and said, "Baby I have missed you all day."

"Yes I am sure, with you free all day, what more would you do but miss me and message me," Ritesh replied.

Riya fumed inside but not wanting to start a fight, she kissed him again, on his neck this time and said, "You missed me too, I know it" and slid her hand into his chest, feeling his body.

Ritesh gave a tired sigh and said, "I am too tired for this. Can't you wait for the weekend?" He went to bed, leaving Riya on the couch alone.

It felt like in one moment, she had it all - admirers, a future in academics and plans for the future. In the other, here she was, stuck all alone at home with a man who had the least interest in her and no future plans for herself. She wanted a friend now more than anything. She suddenly remembered her friend...uhh crush... Suhas. She switched on the app and saw a few 100 more likes on the picture, which was one of the last clicks in Mauritius. She went to the message function and DM'd him, "Looks like someone got too possessive?" and left a wink smiley along with it.

He replied immediately, "I am not the possessive type. But what's mine is mine."

The message sent tingles down her spine. It had been a while since someone had called her mine, or acted like one. She replied "And what is yours?"

His reply was one word, "You."

She sat in silence reading that word. He followed up with a text, "I know many want you, but no one can want you the way I want you. The way I desire you. The way I feel for you. If we meet, you can see the truth in my eyes."

Riya felt another shiver run down her spine. This was too intense and something she didn't want to get into.

She clearly remembered how she had connected with Suhas. Trying to fill her long lonely hours, she had logged into her social media accounts and tried to connect with her old friends from college. She would post some pictures of hers, at regular intervals, which would lead to a lot of appreciation from her friends and slowly growing fans. She started receiving many messages as well, from unknown people appreciating her beauty and sense of fashion. However she would avoid them all.

One day, she saw a DM, from a profile called Suhas, with the cheesiest line ever, "Did I just find love in this hopeless place."

She replied back after some hesitation, "Hahaha. Thanks but I am already taken."

He replied back quickly, "That is because I was not there in your life till now." She laughed at his witty banter and they started conversing. These innocent chats went on for a couple of months where Suhas would say the cheesiest of lines which would make her laugh.

They became friends slowly, but with Riya clearly telling him that she was married and assuming that his cheesy lines were nothing but innocent banter. However, of late she found his messages evoking a desire in her she had not thought of. She would at times spend hours staring at his pictures on Instagram, where he posed stylishly at various locations alone or with his friends. She realized that she had a crush on him.

Ping! Ping! Two more short notifications bought her out of her thoughts. A new DM from the man she was thinking about. "How are you pinging me so late at night? Isn't your husband home now? Isn't this your alone time with him?" asked Suhas.

Torn between telling the truth or acting aloof Riya replied, "Yeah he is back, but he is a bit tired today. So he slept early."

"And it seems you are not tired or ready for bed at all," came back the reply from Suhas.

"Yeah, I have a few minutes before I head back to my bed and my husband," she replied.

"I can live a whole lifetime in a few minute with you, sweetie," he replied.

Unable to control, Riya wrote, "Why are you so damn sweet and romantic all the time?"

"Because you bring out that side of me," he replied.

"I thought I had lost my touch. Or at least with my husband I have," she replied.

"No sweetie, it is he who has lost sense. You are quite sensuous and out of the world. I know he ignores you but you are someone who should be put on a stage not ignored." He replied.

"How do you know he ignores me?" she asked, "Is it so obvious?"

"I could sense your pain and loneliness from the first day we chatted," he replied.

"That's why you have been trying your luck it seems?" she accused.

"My Luck was to be your friend. Anything else will be my fortune," he replied immediately.

Riya was lost for once to his reply. She waited for a moment and replied back, "I don't want to be lonely tonight."

"You are not sweetie. I am here with you," Suhas messaged her back, along with a couple of kiss emojis. Suddenly, emboldened Riya replied with a few Kiss emojis of her own.

"Wow, my first response ever," he replied.

"Well I don't give them lightly. Nor do I ask for them without thinking," she replied back.

"I hope you know what you're doing? Don't play with fire without thinking," he warned her.

"Well you don't know what fire is. The fire that is inside me," she replied back.

"I want to feel the fire and burn in it," he replied back.

"Can you handle it?" she asked.

"Give me a chance and I will satisfy the fire in you," he said.

"Ok!" All she wrote was two words but it conveyed a lot, her willingness, her surrender, her invitation.

"Sweetie, let me kiss you and make you feel better. Let me feel your red lips and give you a taste of mine," he wrote back.

"Yes kiss me, kiss me hard!" she replied.

"Kissing you my love as my hands encircle you in my embrace while my tongue plays with yours," he said.

"I can feel your hands around me. Oh! Suhas, how I miss being touched by desire," she wrote back.

"My lips are tasting yours and my teeth biting your sweet lips, tasting their sweet nectar," he replied.

"Oh! kiss me more… kiss me harder," she texted back.

"Yes I am and my hands are wandering around your body, exploring it," he replied.

Riya was totally turned on by now and she wanted more. She replied in desperation, "Yes, Grab my breast and bite my neck. I really need it."

These words opened the gate for Suhas, as he started with vigor, devouring Riya's body with his mouth and hands, his words painting a graphic and detailed description. Riya knew she had reached a point of no return with Suhas and replied back in kind. "Oh yes Suhas! You make me feel like a woman," replied Riya.

"Let me make you my woman," came back the reply from Suhas.

"Yes, take off my dress, please." moaned Riya.

"Sliding it off while I relish your neck, before I get to your boobs and get to play with your nipples."

Riya could feel herself getting really wet, her nipples hardened under the top she wore. She looked towards the direction of the bedroom, where her husband Ritesh was sleeping. Hearing no noise and seeing a dark room, she assumed he was fast asleep. She slid a hand inside her waistband and slowly reached inside her lace panties, which she had specially worn that night for her husband. She reached into her core and touched her own bud while Suhas sent her words which sparked her imagination and loosened her body lubricants. She plunged inside with her fingers while he kept sending her naughty expressions of his love and admiration. She knew she wanted all that he said to happen in real and she was imagining it with the man who was sending the texts to her. This continued for a few minutes as her finger plunged deep and she came.

Riya said to Suhas, "Darling, thank you for taking care of me. I did not want to feel lonely tonight and you took care of me."

Suhas replied, "I can take care of your loneliness forever. If you give me a chance."

Riya replied, "But I am married and society will frown upon it."

Suhas said, "Ok, then let us at least meet for coffee. I think there is nothing wrong in that?"

Riya said, "I won't be comfortable meeting you at a Starbucks or CCD as there are too many people and someone might know my husband."

Suhas suddenly had an idea, "Ok then let's meet for coffee at a hotel. The crowd there will be more exclusive. So less chances of being discovered."

Riya smiled as she thought about it. After some contemplation, she texted him the name of a nearby five star hotel along with the date and time.

Riya was really happy once her husband finally left for the day. She got ready soon, wearing a stunning red dress, high heels and big sunglasses to hide her face as she left from her home in a cab for the hotel, which was an hour away in late morning traffic.

She reached the coffee shop well before time and went inside, a figure of grace and beauty, she sat on a seat in the corner which allowed her to see the entrance to the store. She ordered a cappuccino and was checking her phone for notifications just when a handsome young man walked in. Suhas was short in height but well-built, his shoulders powerful and broad. He had an easy going grin and was dressed like an affluent man, totally at ease in these settings.

Suhas looked across the room, waved at her and came over to her table. "You look more beautiful in person than your pictures," were the first words out of his mouth.

"Oh! Come on, you are such an incorrigible flirt," replied Riya.

"Your beauty makes me one," he said as he sat down and ordered a coffee for himself.

They already knew each other, over months of chatting and bonding and their conversation was casual but natural. However they were meeting for the first time and the chemistry between both of them was palpable to everyone including them. They both had fire in their eyes as they looked at each other across the table while sipping coffee. Suddenly Suhas slipped his hand across the table and held her hand and said, "Riya I would cross a thousand kilometres to gaze into your eyes and taste your beautiful lips."

Riya clutched his hand and said, "I think you say that to every beautiful woman you meet," and giggled.

"But no one is as beautiful as you are my love," he replied as he came and sat close to her.

They were now barely across the table, touching each other's body. Riya could feel his body heat and desire barely a few inches from her. She had been missing this from ages, a man who wanted her, desired her. She suddenly reached across the table and kissed him on his lips. Suhas, initially surprised, kissed her back with vigor and succor. He ravished her mouth with his tongue, not letting her pause for even a second. She could feel his want and craving for her just as he could feel her need and desire for him.

Suhas broke the kiss first and said, "Let us get a room and some more privacy, if you want."

Riya nodded demurely and said, "Yes, let's do that." They moved towards the reception, where Suhas spoke with the manager and got an opulent suite for themselves.

As soon as they were shown into the room, Suhas tipped the bellhop and closed the door. As he turned towards her, Riya entwined her hands around his shoulder and they started kissing. Suhas pushed her against the wall and they kissed as they forgot about the world outside and those seconds became an eternity for them.

With his hands all over her body, Suhas pulled her down on the floor while he continued kissing her. Riya lay down with her back on the carpet while Suhas was above her. He kissed her on her forehead and then her lips and gazed into her mesmerizing eyes with intensity. "Don't look at me like that Suhas, you are making my body tingle," moaned Riya.

"So what should I do then? Riya?" asked Suhas.

"Just kiss me all over and make me yours," said Riya in a low voice.

That was all he needed to hear as he started kissing her again, with more intensity this time. His mouth piercing hers as his tongue explored her mouth. His hands moved all over her body, slowly undressing her. His mouth followed his hands as he peeled off her red dress slowly; he kept discovering her body with his mouth. Riya moaned in pleasure as she felt his hot mouth and soft hands exploring her. She was feeling an intense pleasure, something she had never felt before and she knew she wanted more. Suhas undressed himself in a hurried manner, throwing his shirt away as he reached between her legs.

Her lush opening was hidden behind a pair of black panties. His hands slid up her thighs. Her muscles danced under his touch as his fingers curled around the waistband of her panties and pulled them down. He could see her wet opening laid bare in front of him. She could feel the heat of his breath between her legs. He tentatively licked it and felt her moan in pleasure. "How sweet you taste!" he said and plunged in again to explore her flower in the most sensuous manner possible, dragging lips and careful tongue, heat singing through her, pleasure crawling through her belly, spreading through her hips like fingers. His nose brushed her clit and her back arched so sharply he dug his fingers into her thighs to keep her steady. And instead of backing off, instead of letting her breathe, he turned the full attention of his mouth to it, holding tight onto her, following the movement of her hips.

His tongue traced the contour of her cunt, his beard brushing soft against her thighs. Every muscle in her body was flexed and hard against him, against her bonds, the pressure ratcheted uptight and hot in her midsection. She wanted to curl up into a ball, wanted to wrap her arms and legs around him. She wanted his grip to bruise her. She wanted to come so bad she could barely think.

He uncurled one arm from around her hip and she felt his fingers brush her ass, under his chin. His tongue dragged up the length of her lips, fingers following the trail. Riya moaned when his fingers found her clit and teased the hard nub. He inserted his index finger into her opening and met the wet warmth. He pushed his finger deep and at the same time sucked on her clit into his mouth. Her cry was sharp and loud and made her acutely aware of the near-silence in the room, of the sounds he was making, the sounds she was making, but he hummed again and smiled against her cunt. He felt her wetness surround his finger as her inner muscles gripped it tight. It turned into a gasp when he thrust two fingers deep into her core. He flipped his hand over, palm up and curled his fingers. "My god," Riya whined.

Sucking over her bud in a rhythmic motion, he was driving her wild. She squirmed, gasping for breath and losing it the next second. He brought her to the edge of ecstasy and she willed it to consume her. She lost her mind, pleading for him not to stop. She grabbed his head moaning loudly. He didn't stop until she came hard and wild. Before she could let go, he moved to her heat and licked the cream up that she'd already released.

Riya was lying languidly on the floor, but Suhas was bursting for some relief. He picked her up suddenly and moved to bed in a hurry. He managed to lay Riya on the bed and was all over her. Riya did not know what to do. She was swept away by the passion of the love she was experiencing. Suhas then took off his pants as Riya was admiring his well-toned body. He placed her hand on his dick and immediately Riya started rubbing it while she kissed his lips. Meanwhile, Suhas started squeezing her boobs and kissing them with his lips that lead to sucking on her hard nipple, flicking it with his tongue. She let out a little gasp of pleasure, realizing she had been digging her nails into his back. She felt his hardening manhood pressed against her stomach as he bent over her kissing her harder.

Riya slid her hands to the front of his shoulder, pushing him back into the bed, licking his neck, his chest, his torso, sliding her hands down along with her tongue. She slid her hands up his legs, and thighs. Suhas grabbed her hair as she got closer to his cock, moaning and fully aroused. She wrapped her fingers around his hard length. Using both hands, she began to stroke up and down his cock again, marveling at the dichotomy of something so soft yet so hard at the same time. She traced the heavy bluish vein that ran the length of his shaft, tracing it from base to the head and back again, cupping his balls with care as she explored with her hands for a moment. He was so big, so hot. She couldn't wait to feel him explode in her mouth. She started sucking at the base of the penis to the end of his shaft; also she was flickering with the tongue in between.

She slowly worked her way back up, hand on the base of your penis. She licked the slit at the tip of his cock, tasting his salty and musky essence. As she continued to circle the head, licking, sucking and gliding, he moaned. She increased her pace with her hand, sliding up and down, at the same time she was sucking and swirling the tip, hollowing her cheeks and sucking harder and flicking his wrist around the base of his length. Suhas started to moan louder than ever, his hips bucking against her.

He tensed and began to pant a little. His hands, which had been moving through her hair, suddenly stopped and she could feel the muscles of his legs tighten around her. Within seconds he had stiffened completely, putting all his weight on his feet and thrusting his hips up in the air, driving his cock deeper into her throat. He made a strangled gurgling sound and then hot streams of cum began pumping down the back of her throat. His eyes squeezed shut and his head threw back in ecstasy.

Riya was lying on the edge of the bed, her pussy wet, but she knew Suhas was spent. She looked at him with a wanting desire in her eyes and saw that he was bouncing back, quick. She extended her hand and started rubbing his cock with her hands, as he got harder. Soon Riya had Suhas ready and erect for her. Riya smiled again and held up her arms for him to hold her. Suhas crawled on top of her, into her arms, and began kissing her lightly on the lips. Riya felt his massive penis throbbing against the skin of her belly as he moved his arms in position around her back, under the bra strap on her back.

"Can you put it inside me?" she asked, freeing herself from his kiss.

Suhas nodded and extricated his lower body from hers. He began positioning his pelvis so as to enter her. Riya took his erection in her right hand and with her left hand, she stretched her pussy lips open as far as she could. She pulled his tool towards her until his tip met the opening of her pussy. His manhood twitched as it entered her. It wasn't enough – Riya's crotch wanted the monster-penis inside it but his dick seemed to be too large to enter her completely. "God, you are so wet," Suhas said, breathlessly.

"Push it in, fast, please," Riya begged. Her pussy was pounding with anticipation, asking for something to fill it swiftly. Suhas backed up a little and thrust hard with his penis, pushing it in a couple of centimeters inside her. Riya squealed, feeling both pain and pleasure as Suhas's penis stretched her pussy open like it had never been stretched before.

"Keep… pushing," Riya whispered, panting.

Suhas obliged, slowly pushing his penis inside her. Riya felt her walls slowly expand and accept his massive organ inside her. She felt him throb as it moved inside her. It took almost a minute for Suhas's penis to be almost fully inside her. "Comfortable?" Suhas asked her, looking into her eyes, his face a few centimeters above hers.

"Yes," Riya replied. But before Riya could complete her thought, Suhas thrust hard pushing the rest of his erection inside her. He groaned once he was fully inside her. Riya yelped loudly with delight. Her eyes closed involuntarily and her breath grew ragged, her breasts heaving in and out. She thought she could feel his penis reach somewhere above her navel. It was deeply fulfilling and satisfying to feel it throb inside her.

"You OK, right?" he asked again. Riya opened her eyes and saw that he looked worried. She ran her hands through his hair and nodded.

She tried to speak but breath was hard to come by. "Fuck me," she said, panting, pushing her arms around him, on to his back.

Suhas drew his penis out of her until it was only about two inches in and then slowly pushed it back in, taking his time, holding her tight to himself all the time. Riya moaned in a slow continuous moan till he was fully inside again, forgetting to breathe. Slowly, Suhas extricated his penis again to being only a couple of inches inside her pussy and Riya breathed a lungful in and out quickly. His next thrust was hard and fast and Riya yelled in ecstasy, her pussy feeling like it was on fire and about to explode. Suhas began to lick her neck as he slowly extracted his penis from deep inside her again and Riya breathed in and out, erratically. He rammed her hard again, harder than the last time and Riya moaned even louder.

Suhas began to lick her ear as he slowly moved his pelvis back, moving his penis out. He rammed her hard again, rendering her helpless, this time Riya's entire body shuddered with delight as she whimpered loudly. She tried to take her arms off him during his slow withdrawal motion but her pussy had begun to enjoy his thrusts and pushes. He pushed up from her to allow her to take it off fully, putting his weight on the bed with his arms, keeping his penis immersed fully inside her – all nine inches of it. Riya sat up partially on her elbows to take off her bra but as she did, something exploded inside her.

"CUMMING!" Riya shouted, breathing hard, as her pussy contracted holding on to Suhas's penis as if for dear life for several seconds and her legs pushed involuntarily into the air. She fully expected her pussy to let go immediately but the first contraction lasted the longest she had ever known. Finally, her pussy expanded and Riya felt and heard it release a moderately large gush of gooey fluid out, down her loins. Her pussy contracted again immediately and she felt the rapid thumping pulse in Suhas's penis the strongest she ever had. Her walls expanded and she heard rather than felt her pussy squirt a smaller amount of fluid out again.

"Stay like this!" she half-shouted to Suhas quickly before she felt the third wave take over her body, this one lifting her hips off the bed's surface a few centimeters, in addition to her already raised legs. A fourth wave came and then a fifth and a sixth and a seventh and an eighth and then finally a ninth, before the orgasm became a series of countless small ripples exploding like small matchstick sized flames in her belly, her breasts and her pussy.

When sense returned to her, Riya realized she had been moaning continuously since she didn't know when. Her legs and hips were still raised in the air. Slowly she moved her hips back to the bed, shuddering.

They lay in bed together exhausted in each other's arms. "Riya that was the best experience I ever had. The connection I feel with you is amazing. Tell me you didn't feel the same?" asked Suhas.

"Yes Suhas, it was one of the best. But I am afraid, I need to leave now. It is quite late and I want to reach home before my husband arrives. I don't want him to suspect me, yet." Riya replied as she got up from bed. Suhas got up after her and held her from behind and kissed her neck once again. "Stop Suhas, I am not joking," said Riya sternly as she started picking up her clothes.

Suhas helps Riya clean up and dress up. Riya checked herself in the mirror and left with a promise to meet again soon.

She went down the hotel and got into her cab, which was waiting downstairs. As soon as she was out of eyesight from the hotel, Riya deleted Suhas's contacts and blocked him everywhere. "I definitely do not want the trouble of having a man fall in love with me." She mumbled to herself.

As she switched on her notification, she saw many messages come in. Riya browsed through them and selected the messages by one particular guy, Swaraj. "Ah! Looks like I have found a new Insta-Love for myself," said Riya as she started messaging him.